Vol.
12

Three Kingdoms

Many centuries ago, China was made up of several provinces that frequently waged war with one another for regional supremacy. In 221 BC, the Qin Dynasty succeeded in uniting the warring provinces under a single banner, but the unity was short-lived, only lasting fifteen years. After the collapse of the Qin Dynasty, the Han Dynasty was established in 206 BC, and unity was restored. The Han Dynasty would last for hundreds of years, until the Post-Han Era, when the unified nation once again began to unravel. As rebellion and chaos gripped the land, three men came forward to take control of the nation: Bei Liu, Cao Cao, and Quan Sun. The three men each established separate kingdoms, Shu, Wei, and Wu, and for a century they contended for supremacy. This was known as the Age of the Three Kingdoms.

Written more than six hundred years ago, *Three Kingdoms* is one of the oldest and most seminal works in all of Eastern literature. An epic story spanning decades and featuring hundreds of characters, it remains a definitive tale of desperate heroism, political treachery, and the bonds of brotherhood.

Wei Dong Chen and Xiao Long Liang have chosen to draw this adaptation of *Three Kingdoms* in a manner reminiscent of the ancient Chinese printing technique. It is our hope that the historical look of *Three Kingdoms* will amplify the timelessness of its themes, which are just as relevant today as they were thousands of years ago.

Wagers and Vows

Created by WEI DONG CHEN

Wei Dong Chen, a highly acclaimed and beloved artist, and an influential leader in the "New Chinese Cartoon" trend, is the founder of Creator World in Tianjin, the largest comics studio in China. Recently the Chinese government entrusted him with the role of general manager of the Beijing Book Fair, and his reputation as a pillar of Chinese comics has brought him many students. He has published more than three hundred cartoons, which have been recognized for their strong literary value not only in Korea, but in Europe and Japan as well. Free spirited and energetic, Wei Dong Chen's positivist philosophy is reflected in the wisdom of his work. He is published serially in numerous publications while continuing to conceive projects that explore new dimensions of the form.

Illustrated by XIAO LONG LIANG

Xiao Long Liang is considered one of Wei Dong Chen's greatest students. One of the most highly regarded cartoonists in China today, Xiao Long's fantastic technique and expression of Chinese culture have won him the acclaim of cartoon lovers throughout China. His other works include "Outlaws of the Marsh" and "A Story on the Motorbike".

Original Story
"The Romance of the Three Kingdoms" *by Luo, GuanZhong*

Editing & Designing
Design Hongs, Jonathan Evans, KH Lee, YK Kim,
HJ Lee, JS Kim, Lampin, Qing Shao, Xiao Nan Li, Ke Hu

Original Chinese edition published by Anhui Fine Arts Publishing House.

Characters

BEI LIU

Bei Liu is one of the three most powerful men in all of China. He has spent years wandering the land in search of a home from which he can base his campaign to restore the Han Dynasty, and now he has established a foothold in JingZhou, a highly coveted territory. But his newfound power has come with many hard choices, and Bei Liu must decide how to manage his alliance with Quan Sun while still fighting Cao Cao. Additionally, can Bei forgive his sworn brother for betraying him? And what of the strange proposal from Quan Sun?

LIANG ZHUGE

Liang Zhuge is the foremost military strategist and logistical thinker in China. Since joining Bei Liu, he has helped his master achieve many victories in battle and win the hearts of the people he rules. Now, Liang Zhuge's mind must be applied to keeping his master one step ahead of his enemies, and two steps ahead of his allies.

YU GUAN

Yu Guan is a famous warrior whose fierceness in battle and fidelity to Bei Liu are the stuff of legend – which makes it all the more remarkable that Yu Guan failed to kill Cao Cao when ordered to do so. Yu Guan's betrayal will test the strength of his blood oath with Bei Liu, as well as the wisdom of Liang Zhuge.

QUAN SUN

Quan Sun is the ruler of Eastern Wu, whose recent victory at ChiBi ("Red Cliffs") should have put him well on his way to claiming the throne. But wars are not decided overnight, and, when Quan Sun sees that Bei Liu has achieved more after the battle than he has, he devises a desperate strategy for luring his ally into a trap from which he will never escape.

YU ZHOU

Yu Zhou commanded Quan Sun's victorious forces at the Battle of the Red Cliffs, and is celebrating his achievement with an enormous banquet. After the festivities, Yu Zhou sets out to claim NanJun fortress, in an effort to one day take JingZhou from Bei Liu. But his attempt fails, leaving Quan Sun with no gains after the battle. It is then that Yu Zhou and Quan Sun hatch a plan to kill Bei Liu.

LADY WU

Lady Wu is the late Jian Sun's second wife and Quan Sun's mother. When Lady Wu hears word of Quan Sun's offer to let Bei Liu marry her daughter as a means of luring him into a trap, she becomes enraged. Since word of the wedding has already spread throughout the land, Lady Wu insists the wedding take place and demands to meet her future son-in-law in person.

Characters

Volume 12

CAO CAO

Cao Cao is the prime minister of China, who recently suffered a humiliating defeat to Quan Sun's forces at the Red Cliffs. While escaping from that battle, Cao Cao is cornered by Yu Guan, Bei Liu's sworn brother. Even though he is under orders to kill Cao Cao, Yu Guan spares him as a way of honoring his pledge to always remember Cao Cao's generosity to him when he thought Bei Liu had been killed.

PI CAO

Pi Cao is Cao Cao's second and most ambitious son, whose goal is to one day take over for his father. Pi's younger brother, Zhi, is a renowned poet whose indifference to power and ability with words provokes a bit of envy in Pi. Nevertheless, Pi Cao looks down on his brother and those he associates with.

YI SIMA

Yi Sima is a former servant of Cao Cao's who has since become a senior consultant to Pi Cao. While his belief that Bei Liu was the true winner at the Red Cliffs earns him ridicule, the assessment is an accurate one and will benefit him later on.

XUAN HAN

Xuan Han is the Governor of ChangSha, a neighboring district to JingZhou. When Yu Guan is sent to conquer ChangSha, Xuan Han leads a stubborn defense of his territory. But his vehemence in battle causes him to doubt his own troops, a choice that will have lethal consequences for him.

ZHONG HUANG

Zhong Huang is a much-admired and venerable soldier who is known to be one of history's greatest archers. While fighting with Bei Liu during the siege of ChangSha, Zhong Huang extends his adversary certain courtesies not seen in battle for years. This arouses the suspicion of his master, who accuses him of helping the enemy.

YAN WEI

Yan Wei is a commander in Xuan Han's army. When his master accuses Zhong Huang of helping the enemy and sentences him to death, Yan Wei decides to take matters into his own hands and root out the true villain in ChangSha.

Chapter 1

The Aftermath of the Red Cliffs 208 AD

Summary

Following the Battle of the Red Cliffs, Cao Cao is desperately trying to escape with his life when he is confronted by Yu Guan. Despite pledging to Bei Liu that he would get rid of Cao Cao, Yu Guan spares his life as a means of thanking him for his kindness years before. Cao Cao returns home, where he wallows in self-pity before recommitting himself to winning the war.

Meanwhile, Yu Zhou is throwing a victory celebration in Eastern Wu. Over many drinks and toasts, Yu Zhou honors all who have helped him, living and dead. At the end of the night, he learns that Bei Liu plans to attack NanJun Fortress as means of taking full control of JingZhou.

Yu Guan is brought before Bei Liu and Liang Zhuge for failing to kill Cao Cao. Liang Zhuge orders him to be beheaded for the crime, but Bei Liu intervenes and spares Yu Guan's life. Liang Zhuge, who never truly planned to kill Yu Guan, tells Bei Liu that his fidelity to his sworn brother will pay off when Yu Guan is asked to repay the mercy.

Later, Yu Zhou arrives in JingZhou to ask about the attack on NanJun. Liang Zhuge says they would only attack if Yu Zhou fails to claim it for his own, after which Yu Zhou carelessly says that Bei Liu can have it if the Wu general doesn't claim it in a day's time.

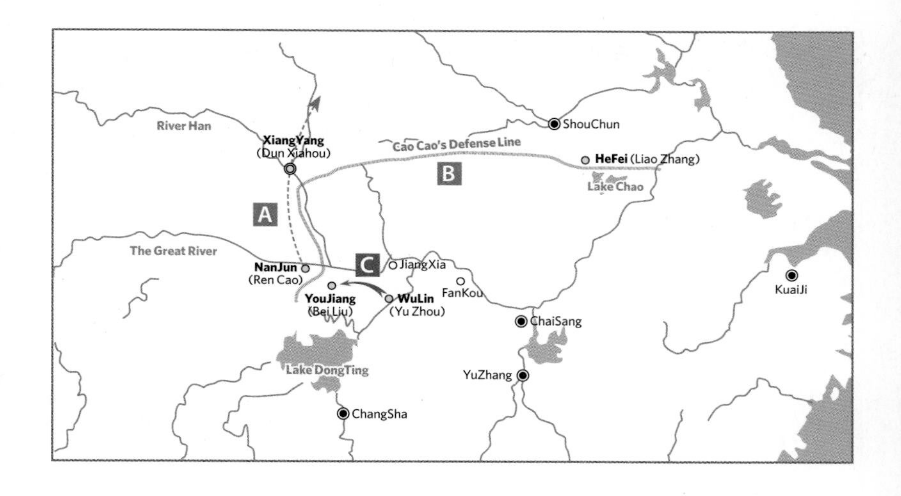

A Cao Cao escapes from the Red Cliffs and returns to XuChang.

B Once home, Cao Cao orders Ren Cao, Dun XiaHou, and Liao Zhang to defend his holdings.

C Yu Zhou visits Bei Liu in YouJiang and warns him against attacking NanJun.

GREETINGS, MY LORD. YOU LOOK EXHAUSTED. YOURS HAS BEEN A LONG, AGONIZ-ING JOURNEY THROUGH DARKNESS.
ALLOW ME TO EASE YOUR PAIN FOR GOOD.

HEH... I SHOULD HAVE KNOWN.
I WAS WONDERING WHEN I WOULD SEE YOU, YU GUAN.
I THOUGHT IT WOULD BE SOONER.
BUT IT SEEMS YOU ARE MY FINAL OPPONENT.

THIS WAS NOT HOW I IMAGINED IT WOULD TURN OUT, EITHER.
I SUSPECT IT WAS FATED TO END LIKE THIS.
THE WILL OF THE HEAVENS.
TAKE HEART. THIS IS BIGGER THAN EITHER OF US.

IT SEEMS THE WORLD WOULD LIKE TO THINK OF ME AS A VILLAINOUS HERO.

BUT I DID WHAT I SWORE TO DO!
AND I HAVE ALWAYS ACTED WITH CONSISTENT HONOR!

YET THIS IS THE REWARD I GET...
TO BE KILLED BY THE MAN I ADMIRE MOST IN THE WORLD.

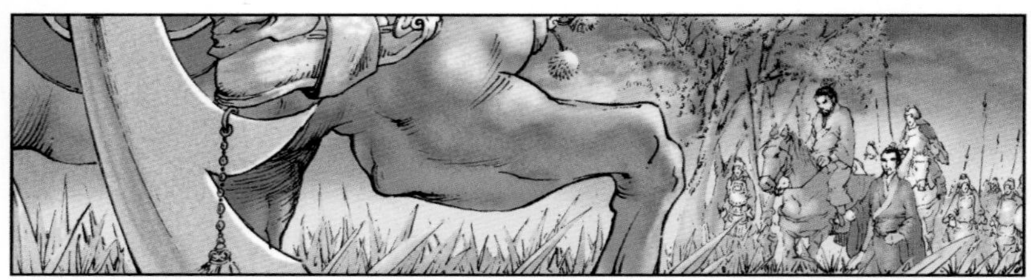

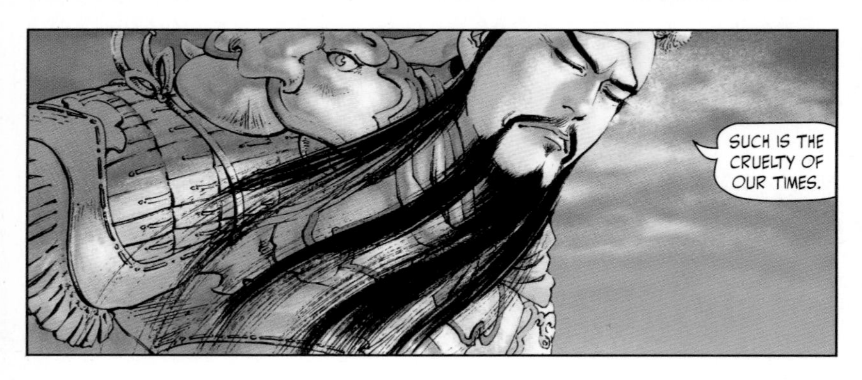
SUCH IS THE CRUELTY OF OUR TIMES.

MY LORD, PLEASE! I BEG YOU, DON'T DO THIS! HAVE YOU FORGOTTEN HOW CAO CAO WAS KIND TO YOU WHEN YOU NEEDED HIM?
I FOUGHT FOR HIM IN BATTLE AND WON. I SHED BLOOD FOR HIM. MY DEBT IS REPAID.

WHAT ABOUT THE TIME YOU KILLED SIX OF HIS BORDER GUARDS ON YOUR WAY TO THE YELLOW RIVER. THAT WAS A CRIME PUNISHABLE BY DEATH! BUT STILL HE LET YOU GO.
YOU SAID YOU'D BE FOREVER GRATEFUL. THIS ISN'T ABOUT A DEBT. IT'S ABOUT YOUR HONOR!

HOW DARE YOU--

ENOUGH OF THIS!
YU GUAN'S HONOR IS BEYOND QUESTION.

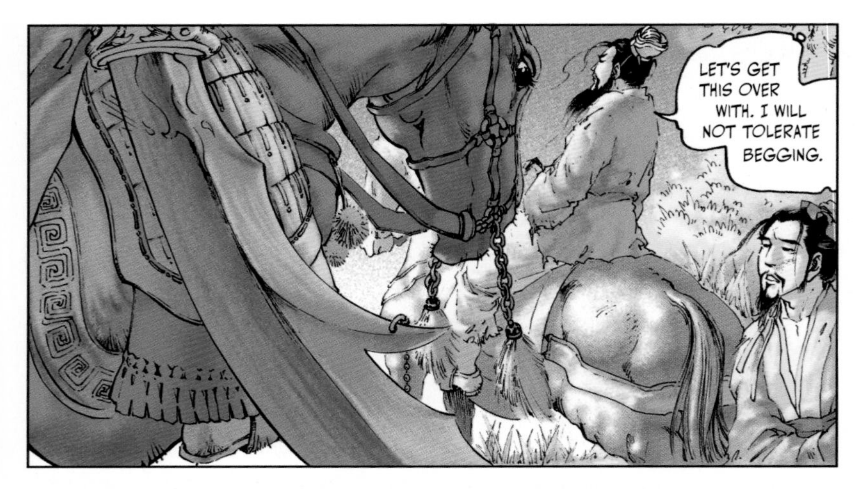
LET'S GET THIS OVER WITH. I WILL NOT TOLERATE BEGGING.

YU GUAN, LET IT BE KNOWN THAT I HAVE NO REGRETS.
IT IS AN HONOR TO DIE BY YOUR HAND.

≡ SIGH ≡

STOP CRYING. YOU MAY PASS.

LEAVE, NOW! BEFORE I CHANGE MY MIND!

MY LORD, LET'S GO.

CAO CAO'S CAMP

...

SOB

I CAN'T... I DON'T...
SOB

WHY?
TELL ME THAT!
BAM
BAM

SOB
WHY?!!!

MY LORD, PLEASE.
YOU'VE NEVER LOST HEART BEFORE. NOT AT THE RED CLIFFS. NOT AT WULIN. WHY DO YOU WEEP NOW?

JIA GUO!
DON'T YOU GET IT? THIS IS ALL BECAUSE OF JIA GUO. SINCE HIS DEATH, NOTHING HAS BEEN THE SAME!

!
OOO

IF HE'D LIVED, THE SCHEMES OF YU ZHOU AND LIANG ZHUGE WOULDN'T TROUBLE US.
BUT HE DIDN'T, AND LOOK AT WHERE WE ARE!

I'VE BEEN REDUCED TO BEGGING FOR MY LIFE LIKE SOME KIND OF COMMON THIEF.

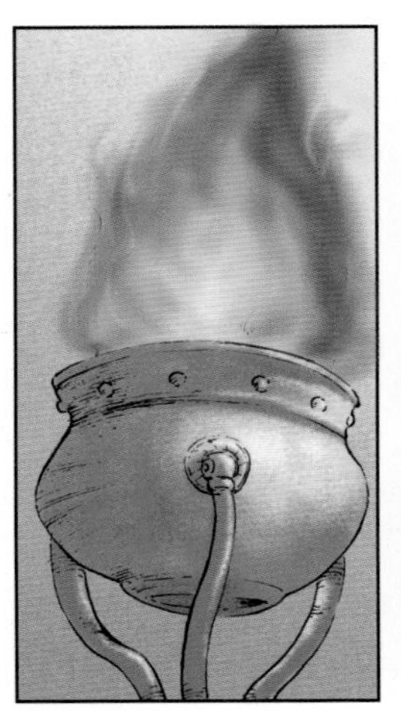

SNFF
I'M SORRY.
THIS MOOD WILL PASS. I REFUSE TO FEEL SORRY FOR MYSELF ALL THE TIME.

MY LORD, A REPORT FOR YOU.

HERE ARE THE NUMBERS FROM THE RED CLIFFS.
WE WENT INTO BATTLE WITH ALMOST A MILLION MEN.
TAKING INTO ACCOUNT THOSE WHO ARE DEAD, WOUNDED, MISSING, OR BEING HELD CAPTIVE... WE HAVE ROUGHLY 200,000 SOLDIERS LEFT.

THE BAD NEWS IS THAT OUR NAVAL FORCES HAVE BEEN COMPLETELY ANNIHILATED. THE GOOD NEWS IS THAT THE QINGZHOU ARMY IS STILL INTACT.
HEH.
I ALWAYS KNEW THE QINGZHOU ARMY WAS THE BEST OF OUR RANKS.

WE'VE ALSO RETAINED ALMOST ALL OF OUR SUPPLIES AND LAND, AND OUR CAVALRY IS COMPLETELY INTACT.
SO FOR RIGHT NOW, WE STILL HAVE SUFFICIENT RESOURCES FOR FIGHTING.
AND THE CENTRAL DISTRICTS ARE WELL STOCKED, SO WE'LL QUICKLY RECOUP WHATEVER WE'VE LOST.

YOU SEE, MY LORD? DESPITE OUR DEFEAT, WE REMAIN STRONG. WE MUST LAUNCH A COUNTER-ATTACK RIGHT AWAY! THE ENEMY WOULD NEVER EXPECT IT!

NO. THIS IS NOT THE TIME. QUAN SUN'S FORCES ARE TOO EMBOLDENED RIGHT NOW. WE MUSTN'T GET AHEAD OF OURSELVES.
BESIDES, BEI LIU HAS SPENT THIS TIME BUILDING UP HIS OWN FORCES TO CONQUER OUR LANDS.

OUR FOCUS RIGHT NOW MUST BE ON DEFENDING WHAT'S OURS, NOT LAUNCHING ANOTH-ER ATTACK.

I WILL RETURN TO XUCHANG, WHERE I WILL FOCUS ON REBUILDING OUR FORCES.

REN CAO, STAY HERE AND DEFEND JINGZHOU.

DUN XIAHOU, I AM PUTTING XIANGYANG UNDER YOUR PROTECTION.

LIANG ZHANG, I'M SURE QUAN SUN WILL PERSONALLY LEAD AN ARMY TO ATTACK HEFEI.

TAKE DIAN LI AND JIN YUE. YOU MUST KEEP HEFEI, NO MATTER WHAT!

HOLD THESE LANDS WHILE I REGAIN MY FOOTING. YOU MUST NOT FAIL.
YES, MY LORD.

QUAN SUN'S CAMP
WHO WOULD LIKE TO MAKE A TOAST?
I WILL! TO EASTERN WU'S PERFECT VICTORY!

TONIGHT, WE SALUTE ONE ANOTHER!
BUT THIS VICTORY BELONGS NOT ONLY TO US, BUT THE ENTIRE WU PROVINCE!

AH!
NOW LET ME MAKE A TOAST. TO COMMANDER YU ZHOU!
THANKS TO HIM, WE REDUCED AN ARMY OF ONE MILLION TO ASHES PRACTICALLY OVERNIGHT!

I WOULD CONSIDER IT AN HONOR TO POUR YOUR DRINK.

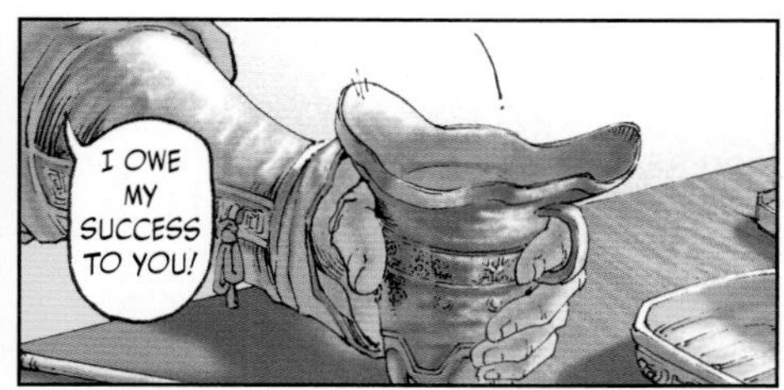
I OWE MY SUCCESS TO YOU!

I'M FLATTERED, MY LORD. BUT DON'T FORGET, I WOULD HAVE ACHIEVED NOTHING IN BATTLE HAD YOU NOT PUT ME IN CHARGE.
YOUR TRUST MADE THIS POSSIBLE. I SHOULD POUR A DRINK FOR YOU.

VERY WELL. TO US!
WHO ELSE HAS A TOAST?

MY LORD!
AH, YES! MY FRIENDS...

COMMANDER GUI HUANG, YOUR COUNTER-ATTACK WAS ONE OF THE DEFINING MOMENTS OF THE BATTLE. IT WAS BOLD, RECKLESS, AND BRILLIANT!
BUT YOU SUSTAINED SERIOUS INJURIES IN THE PROCESS. FOR THIS, I TAKE FULL BLAME.

AS PUNISHMENT, I DRINK TO HONOR YOU! HA HA!

GULP

MY LORD, I MAY HAVE SUSTAINED INJURIES, BUT I WAS LAUGHING THROUGH THE PAIN THE WHOLE TIME. I WAS LAUGHING BECAUSE I KNEW WE WERE THRASHING CAO CAO'S FORCES!
IT WAS AN HONOR TO BE ASKED, AND FOR THAT I TOAST TO YOU!

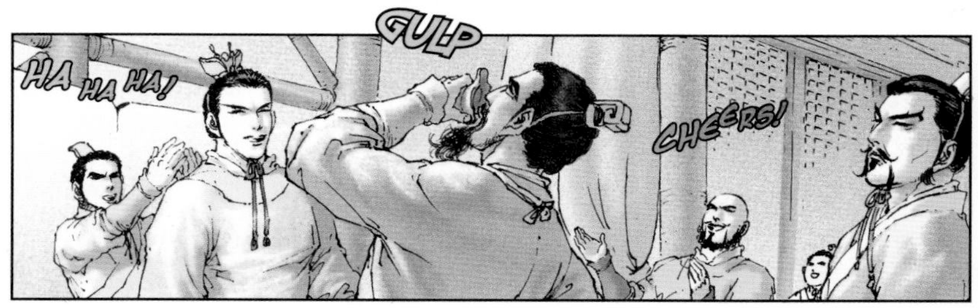
GULP
HA HA HA!
CHEERS!

ALL OF YOU, IF I MAY... OUR TRIUMPH TODAY IS ONE FOR THE AGES, BUT IT DOES NOT BELONG TO US ALONE.
THERE ARE OTHERS WE MUST HONOR.
WE MUST HONOR THE MEMORY OF THE LEADERS WE LOST, WHOSE SACRIFICES MADE THIS DAY POSSIBLE.
I PROPOSE A TOAST TO THE MEMORY OF THE EASTERN TIGER, JIAN SUN, AND HIS SON, THE GREAT CONQUEROR CE SUN.

TO THE FAMILY SUN!
TO EASTERN WU!

NOW, EACH OF YOU ARE WELCOME TO CELEBRATE TO YOUR HEART'S CONTENT. BUT THERE IS SOMETHING TO REMEMBER...
THIS IS THE END OF THE BATTLE, BUT NOT THE WAR. AND THIS IS ONLY THE FIRST STEP TOWARD A NEW AND BETTER WORLD.
OUR ENEMIES REMAIN AT LARGE AND ARE PLOTTING THEIR REVENGE. WE HAVE BEEN THROUGH MUCH TOGETHER, BUT WE MUST REMAIN STRONG AND FINISH THIS.

DESTROYING CAO CAO MEANS WE WILL HAVE REDRAWN THE MAP OF THE WORLD.
WITH EASTERN WU RIGHT AT THE CENTER OF IT!
REST ASSURED, WE WILL REMAIN STRONG!
TO THE NEW WORLD!

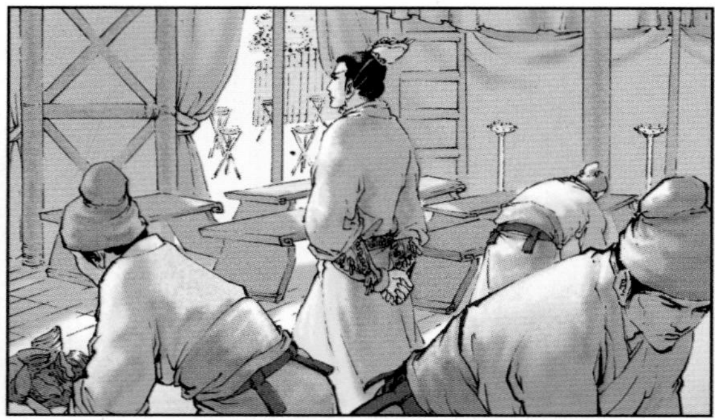

MY LORD!

WE'VE JUST RECEIVED SOME BAD NEWS. BEI LIU HAS PLACED HIS FORCES AROUND NANJUN!

JUST AS I EXPECTED HE WOULD.
HE'S TRYING TO CONQUER JINGZHOU WHILE OUR BACKS ARE TURNED.

WE'VE JUST COME THROUGH A GREAT BATTLE. MAYBE WE SHOULD HOLD BACK FOR NOW.
NO!

THE BATTLE WE'VE JUST COME THROUGH WAS TO STOP CAO CAO'S MASSIVE ARMY FROM TAKING JINGZHOU.

THERE'S NO WAY I'M GOING TO LET BEI LIU WEASEL HIS WAY INTO THE TERRITORY. I'LL DEAL WITH THIS STARTING TOMORROW.

MEANWHILE, IN BEI LIU'S CAMP...
Yu Guan, having allowed Cao Cao to escape at HuaRong Path, was brought before his elders and charged with treason.

YU GUAN!
ALL OF OUR COMMANDERS SERVED HONORABLY AND DEFEATED THE ENEMY FORCES IN EXACTLY THE MANNER THEY WERE ASKED TO. ALL EXCEPT FOR YOU.
YOU NOT ONLY FAILED AT YOUR TASK, YOU ALLOWED CAO CAO TO LIVE. BECAUSE OF YOU, MILLIONS MORE COULD DIE!

WHAT DO YOU HAVE TO SAY FOR YOURSELF?

I HAVE NO DEFENSE FOR MY ACTIONS.
I HAVE BROKEN MY WORD AND DESERVE TO DIE.

SO BE IT.
WE CANNOT MAKE EXCEPTIONS TO THE RULE OF LAW.
TAKE HIM AWAY. EXECUTE HIM WITHIN THE HOUR.

WAIT! DON'T TOUCH HIM!

LIANG ZHUGE, LISTEN TO ME. I SWORE AN OATH TO SHARE THIS MAN'S FATE. I WILL NOT BREAK THAT OATH.
DON'T LET YOUR FEELINGS DECIDE, MY LORD. YOU MUST TREAT EACH OF YOUR MEN EQUALLY. MERCY CAN BE EXPLOITED.

HA! I KNOW THAT BETTER THAN MOST. BUT I WON'T ALLOW YU GUAN TO DIE.

BESIDES, HIS DEBT TO US WILL BE REPAID BY FUTURE ACTIONS.

VERY WELL.

YU GUAN...
YOUR SWORN BROTHER HAS JUST SAVED YOUR LIFE. I WILL FORGIVE THIS INDISCRETION. BUT I EXPECT YOU TO USE YOUR VAUNTED HEROISM TO MORE THAN REPAY THIS KINDNESS.

HE WILL.
HE WILL.

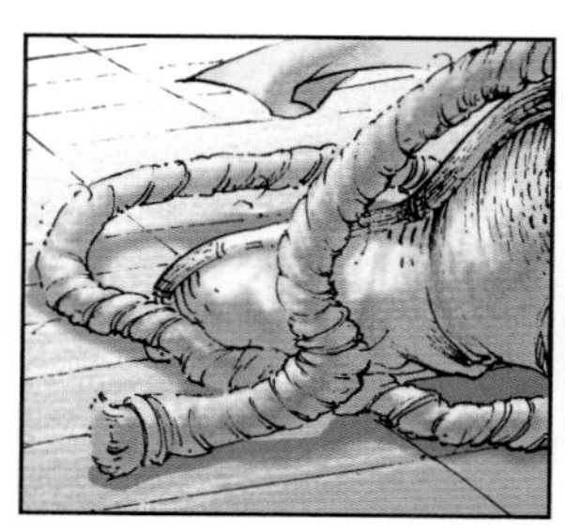

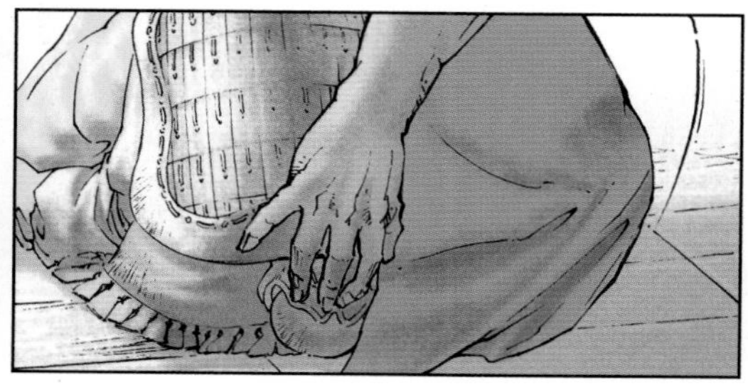

COMMANDER LIANG ZHUGE.

NOT TO WORRY.
SOME TIME AGO, I COULD SENSE THAT CAO CAO WAS GOING TO LIVE FOR A WHILE.
THAT'S WHY I SENT YU GUAN TO CAPTURE HIM.
I OWE YOU. I COULD NO SOONER ALLOW YU GUAN TO DIE THAN I COULD MY OWN FLESH AND BLOOD.

YOU SEE, YU GUAN'S FAILURE TO KILL CAO CAO MEANS THAT HE WILL BE EVEN MORE LOYAL TO YOU THAN HE ALREADY WAS. IN ADDITION, YOUR MERCY AND FIDELITY HAVE BEEN DISPLAYED FOR EVERYONE TO SEE.
SO THIS WAS ALL PART OF YOUR PLAN? I DON'T KNOW WHAT TO SAY.
DON'T SAY ANYTHING. IT'S JUST MY JOB.

GET YOUR HANDS OFF OF ME! WHERE IS THE
MAGGOT WHO DARES THREATEN THE LIFE OF MY SWORN BROTHER?
I DON'T CARE WHAT LIANG ZHUGE'S TITLE IS!
I'M GOING TO GUT HIM LIKE A PIG FOR THIS!

GRR...
BROTHER! WHAT HAS THIS WORTHLESS LOUSE DONE WITH YU GUAN? ANSWER ME!
DON'T TELL ME YOU'VE ALREADY HAD HIM KILLED!
SAY SOME- THING!

WHAT'S DONE IS DONE, FEI ZHANG!
THERE'S NOTHING YOU CAN DO ABOUT IT.
YU GUAN HAS BEEN SPARED AND SENT TO WORK. SO WHY ARE YOU MAKING A SCENE LIKE THIS AFTER THE FACT?!
WAIT.
HUH?
HE...
YOU DIDN'T--
DON'T YOU HAVE AN ARMY TO INSPECT?

YES, I SUPPOSE I DO.

HEY, ALMOST FORGOT, NEWS FROM THE FRONT.
WORD HAS BEEN SENT FROM YU ZHOU. HE INTENDS TO PAY A VISIT, AND SOON.

HEH...

FEI ZHANG, YOU SHOULD GO OUT TO MEET HIM. WE'LL FOLLOW YOUR LEAD.

HA! YOU GOT IT!

SORRY ABOUT THE INTRUSION. I'D HEARD A RUMOR THAT YOU WERE PLANNING TO KILL YU GUAN.
AND WHAT HAVE I TOLD YOU ABOUT ACTING FIRST AND THINKING SECOND?

YU ZHOU MUST WANT TO COMPETE OVER NANJUN.
WHAT SHOULD WE DO?

LET HIM. HE'LL KILL HIMSELF TRYING TO WIN IT. WE JUST NEED TO MAKE SURE THERE'S NOTHING FOR HIM TO WIN.

A short time later, Yu Zhou arrived...

BEI LIU'S ARMY IS BIGGER AND MORE WELL PREPARED THAN WE EXPECTED. THIS WILL NOT BE AS EASY AS WE THOUGHT.
YOU'RE QUITE RIGHT.

MY LORD BEI LIU, I CONFESS I ENVY THE FORCES YOU'VE MUSTERED.
THANK YOU, MY LORD. BUT I'M AFRAID MY FORCES ARE NOWHERE NEAR AS SUPREME AS THE FORCES OF EASTERN WU.

JUDGING BY THE STATE OF YOUR ARMY, I'D SAY YOU HAVE A MIND TO TAKE NANJUN. IS THIS TRUE?
OF COURSE IT'S TRUE!

AS I'M SURE YOU KNOW, I HAVE NOWHERE TO CALL HOME RIGHT NOW. NANJUN WOULD BE PERFECT.

AS I'M SURE YOU KNOW, EASTERN WU IS ALREADY FIGHTING FOR IT.
DO YOU INTEND TO TAKE IT FROM US?

NOT AT ALL. NANJUN IS DEFENDED BY REN CAO. HE IS FORMIDABLE. WE WERE ONLY PLANNING TO FIGHT FOR IT IF YOU FAIL.

HA!
IF WE FAIL? TO BEAT A MAN LIKE REN CAO?
THE SUN WOULD SOONER FAIL TO RISE! TELL YOU WHAT, IF IT TAKES ME MORE THAN A DAY TO CONQUER, YOU CAN HAVE IT.

YOU KNOW, I THINK HE JUST MADE A WAGER.

THIS IS WHY YOU MIND YOUR TONGUE, COMMANDER YU ZHOU...

ALL RIGHT, I ACCEPT YOUR DEAL AND CALL ON LIANG ZHUGE AND SU LU AS WITNESSES.

FINE! DEAL! WHAT DO I HAVE TO WORRY ABOUT?
BUT--
HA HA! WITH ANY LUCK, NOTHING AT ALL.

ALL YOU HAVE TO DO IS WIN NANJUN. IF YOU DO THAT, THEN THIS WAGER WON'T AMOUNT TO ANYTHING.

GET OUR THINGS. WE'RE LEAVING.

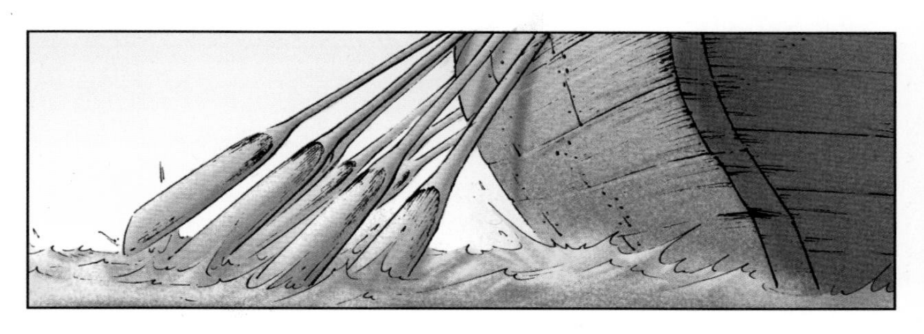

MY LORD, ARE YOU INSANE? THERE'S NO GUARANTEE WE CAN DO THIS. WHY TAKE THAT BET?

OH, CALM DOWN. THE PEOPLE OF NANJUN ARE WAR WEARY. THEY'RE LIKELY TO SURRENDER IF I SO MUCH AS LIFT A FINGER.
WE'LL WIN NANJUN, AND BEI LIU WILL HAVE TO FIND ANOTHER PLACE TO LIVE.

Chapter 2

Bei Liu in JingZhou 209 AD

Summary

Yu Zhou sets out to attack NanJun, and along the way encounters an army commanded by Ren Cao. During the course of fighting, Yu Zhou begins coughing up blood. Thinking he has the upper hand, Ren Cao marches his army directly into a trap, and Yu Zhou is victorious. However, when he reaches NanJun, he finds it already occupied by an army led by Yun Zhao, who says that Yu Zhou lost his bet that he could take it in three days. Realizing he's been outwitted by Liang Zhuge, Yu Zhou collapses and is hospitalized.

Su Lu goes to Liang Zhuge and pleads with him to turn over JingZhou to Quan Sun, but Liang Zhuge insists that, as a member of the royal family, Bei Liu has a right to land owned by the Han Dynasty. When Su Lu tells a recovering Yu Zhou what Liang Zhuge told him, Yu Zhou flies into a rage and orders his men to retaliate.

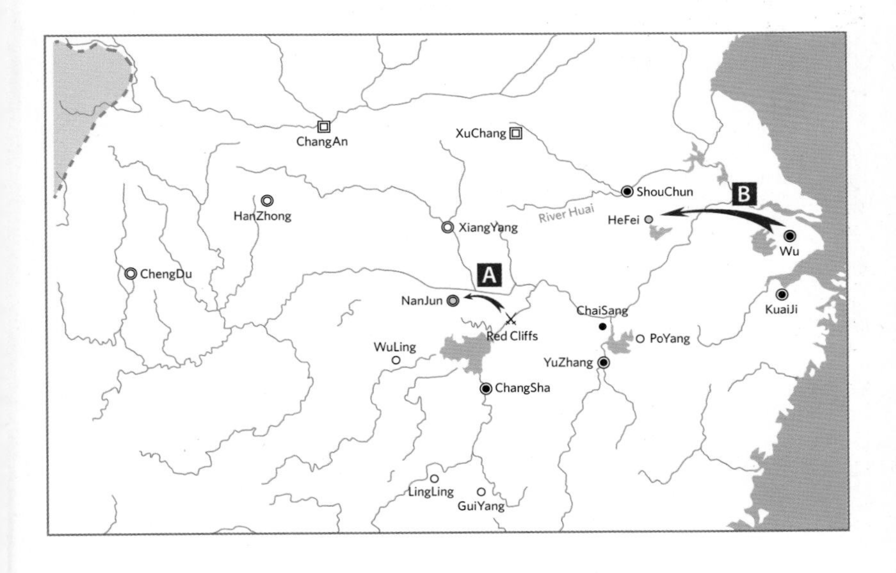

A Yu Zhou does battle with Ren Cao on his way to NanJun.

B Quan Sun mounts an attack against HeFei, defended by Liao Zhang.

LATER, AFTER MUCH FIGHTING BETWEEN YU ZHOU AND REN CAO...
REN CAO

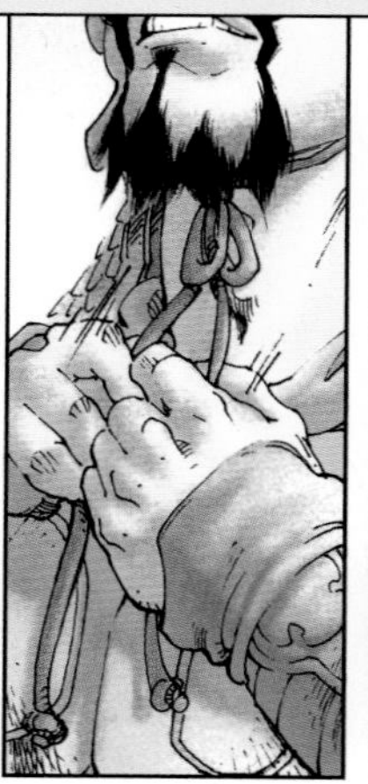

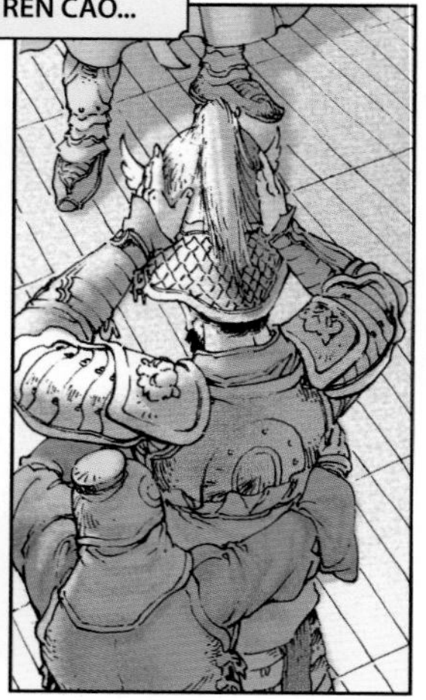

PHEW
HE IS TOUGH.
I WAS SURE I'D CAPTURE YU ZHOU IN THAT AMBUSH.
IF I HAD DONE IT, I COULD HAVE KILLED HIM.
THIS SHOULD BE OVER BY NOW. I MUST DO BETTER.

I'M TOO ANXIOUS TO REST LONG.

GULP

SO...

YU ZHOU SURVIVED THE DAY, BUT HE IS INJURED. SO WE SHALL NOT LET UP. THE NEXT ATTACK WILL BE TOMORROW.

VERY WELL. IT'S A TOUGH, BUT WISE, CHOICE. THE LONGER THIS BATTLE DRAGS ON, THE FEWER OPPORTUNITIES WE HAVE FOR VICTORY.
I AGREE.
HONG CAO

MEANWHILE, IN YU ZHOU'S CAMP...
STEP ASIDE! I MUST INSPECT THE FORCES MYSELF!
BE CALM, MY LORD.

YU ZHOU, YOU ARE WOUNDED. YOU MUST REST. THE BATTLE CAN WAIT.

DON'T BE FOOLISH! THE ENEMY IS PLANNING ITS NEXT ATTACK WHILE WE SPEAK! WHY SHOULD I REST WHEN THEY WON'T?
BECAUSE THEIR PLAN IS TO GRIND YOU DOWN.

THEY KNOW YOU ARE WOUNDED. SO THEY CONTINUE TO PROVOKE YOU. THEIR GOAL IS TO MAKE YOUR INJURY WORSE, SO THAT IT WILL KILL YOU.

BACK OFF! YOU THINK ONE ARROW CAN KILL ME?

I WILL NOT ALLOW MY INJURY TO AFFECT OUR PLANS!
I WOULD LOOK WEAK IF I DID. THIS IS ABOUT PERCEPTION.

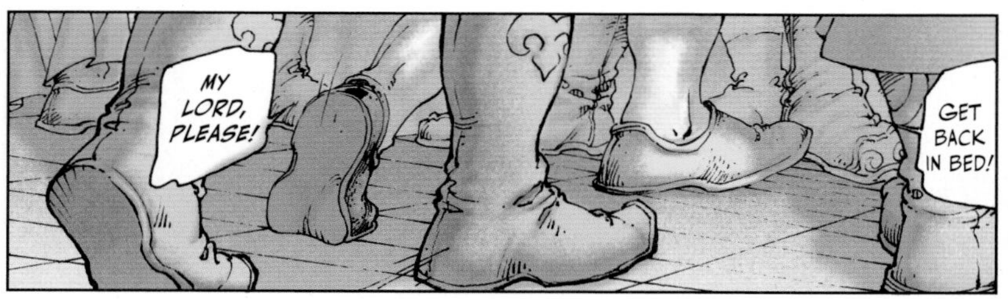
MY LORD, PLEASE!
GET BACK IN BED!

ENOUGH! WHAT IS THE MATTER WITH YOU?
I'M THE MAN WHO DESTROYED CAO CAO'S ARMY!

YOU THINK I CAN'T BEAT REN CAO?
I EAT BIGGER FISH FOR BREAKFAST! NOW STOP WHINING AND START FOLLOW-ING ORDERS!

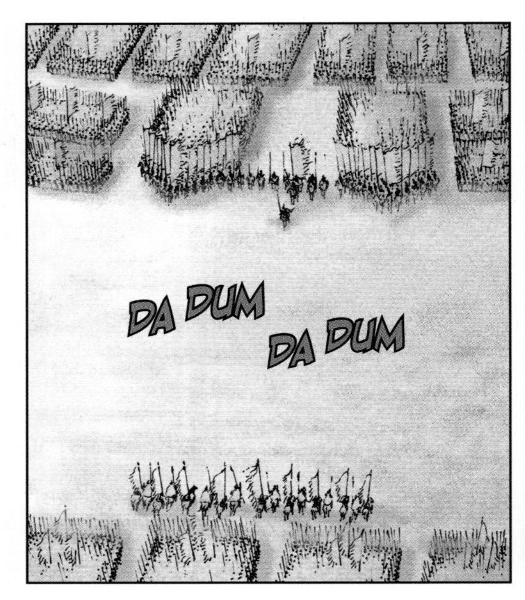
DA DUM
DA DUM

YU ZHOU!
SO GLAD YOU COULD MAKE IT OUT TODAY.

WE WERE WORRIED. THE NEWS WAS THAT YOUR INJURY WAS TOO MUCH FOR YOU TO HANDLE.
WE WERE AFRAID YOU WOULDN'T FIGHT. THAT YOU'D RATHER STAY IN YOUR KITCHEN, COOKING FOR YOUR MEN! HA!

CLOP CLOP

I WOULDN'T LET YOU DOWN, REN CAO. YOU WANT ME? YOU GOT ME.

NOW I WILL REWARD YOUR EAGERNESS BY SENDING YOU ON A FAST JOURNEY TO HELL!

SHOOMP

FZZZ
HMPH.

TONK

PLONK

SHUSHUSHU

HA HA HA! NOT THE WORST SHOT I'VE SEEN. TELL ME, DID YOUR HUSBAND TEACH YOU HOW TO FIRE AN ARROW? PERHAPS YOU COULD SEND HIM OUT IN YOUR PLACE!
THEN YOU CAN RETURN HOME TO YOUR COOKING AND KNITTING!

HA HA HA HA!

HOW DARE YOU...

GRUH!
MY LORD, WHAT'S WRONG?
HE'S COUGHED UP BLOOD!
HA HA HA!

YOU SEE? THE BATTLE IS TOO MUCH FOR HIS DELICATE FEATURES. CHARGE!

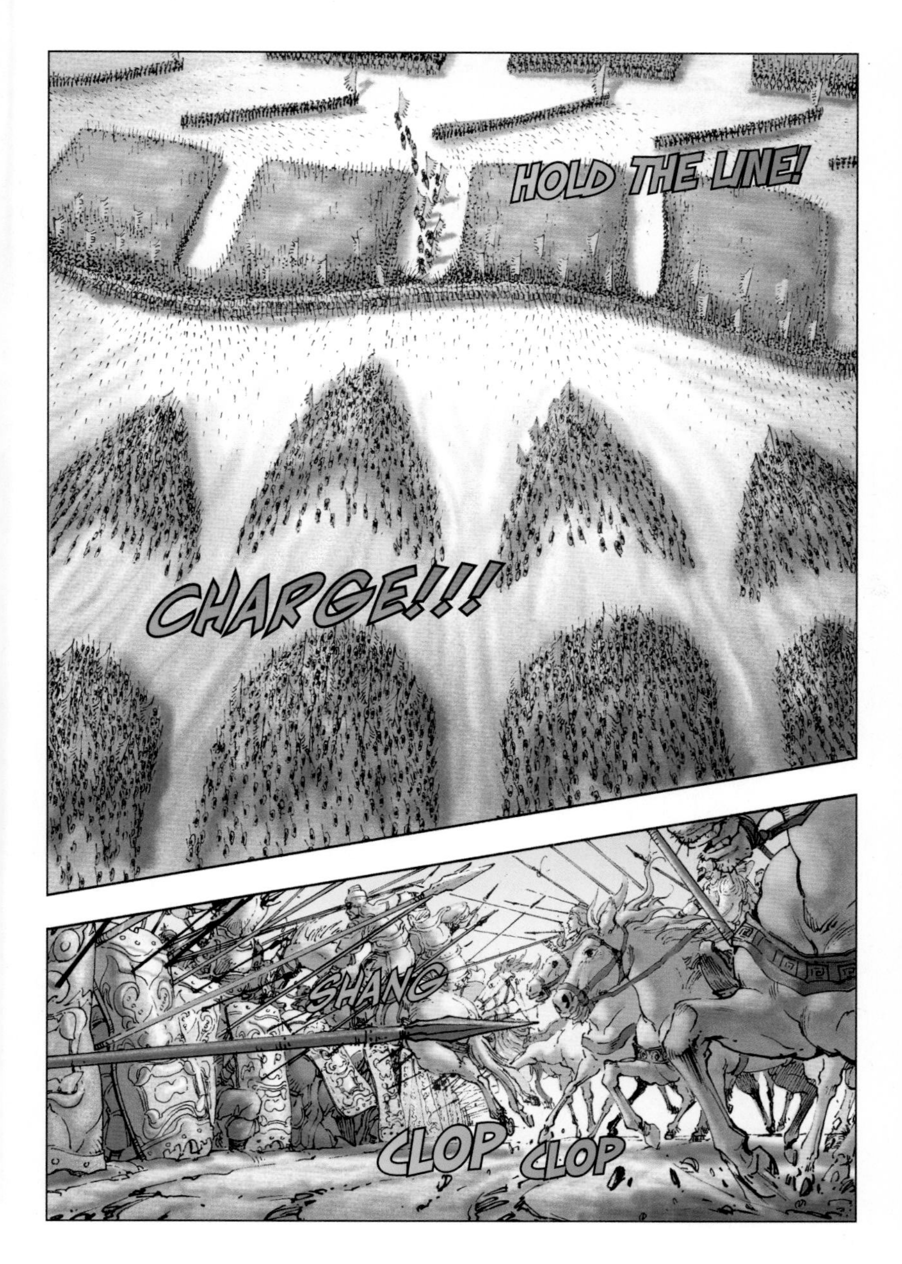
HOLD THE LINE!
CHARGE!!!
SHANG
CLOP CLOP

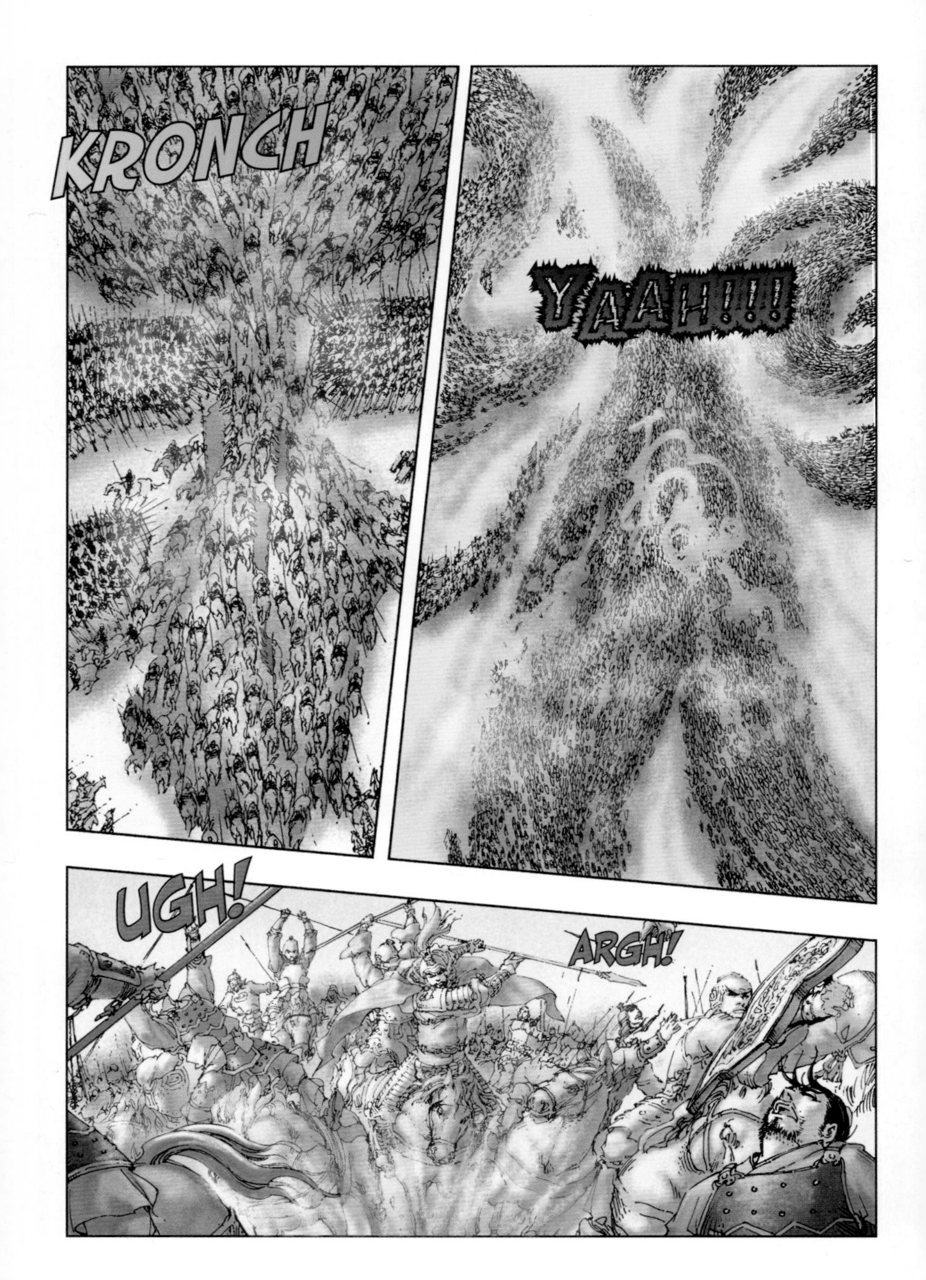
KRONCH
YAAH!!!
UGH!
ARGH!

KEEP CHARGING! INTO THE ENEMY CAMP!
FLATTEN ANYTHING THAT MOVES IN THERE!
CLOP CLOP
YAAH!!!
BA DUM
BA DUM

VICTORY IS SO CLOSE I CAN TASTE IT!
HA!
THE ONLY THING SWEETER WOULD BE THE TASTE OF YU ZHOU'S BLOOD!
CHARGE!!!
?
CLOP CLOP

WAIT, WHAT'S GOING ON?
THE CAMP IS EMPTY.
THERE'S NO ONE HERE, MY LORD.
EMPTY? IT'S A TRAP!
FALL BACK! GET OUT OF HERE!

EH?
FWIZZ

HAWOOOSH
AIIIE!
FWIZZ

YOU SEE? I TOLD YOU THIS WAS ALL ABOUT PERCEPTION. NOW WHO'S WOUNDED?
A VERY CLEVER SCHEME. NOW WE CAN CLAIM NANJUN.

A SHORT TIME LATER...

CITIZENS OF NANJUN, OPEN YOUR GATE! YU ZHOU IS HERE TO TAKE OVER!

SHUNK

!

MY LORD! LOOK AT THOSE FLAGS! THEY'RE BEI LIU'S!

WELCOME, COMMANDER YU ZHOU! IT'S GOOD TO SEE YOU.
BUT I'M AFRAID YOU'VE COME TOO LATE. WE HAVE CLAIMED NANJUN IN YOUR ABSENCE. IF I WERE YOU, I'D MOVE ON.
YUN ZHAO

YU ZHOU
MOVE ON?
DON'T BE SUCH AN IDIOT!
I WON THIS CITY, AND I'VE COME TO TAKE WHAT'S MINE!

I DIDN'T LOSE A STUPID BET. I MERELY ACT ON THE ORDERS OF MY MASTER, WHO WON.
YES, BUT IT TOOK YOU LONGER THAN A DAY, DIDN'T IT?

HOW DARE YOU!

CLOP CLOP

I ORDERED YOU TO ATTACK JINGZHOU AND YANGYANG.
WHY ARE YOU STILL HERE?

TONG LING!
NING GAN!

FORGIVE US, MY LORD. LIANG ZHUGE FORGED LETTERS TELLING US TO REMAIN HERE, THAT EVERYTHING WAS UNDER CONTROL.
THEN HE SENT FEI ZHANG AND YU GUAN TO TAKE BOTH CITIES.

THEY'VE ALREADY TAKEN...

GAH!

I... I DON'T BELIEVE... HRRK
In the end, Yu Zhou's wound proved to be more trouble than he had thought, and the news of Liang Zhuge's trickery made it worse. The worsening injury meant that Yu Zhou had to spend the next day in bed.
DAMN YOU, LIANG ZHUGE! GRAHH!

Meanwhile, Su Lu visited Bei Liu, seeking to recover JingZhou.
YOU MUST ADMIT, THIS CAN'T GO ON.

I WAS ONLY BARELY ABLE TO CONVINCE YU ZHOU NOT TO GO TO WAR WITH YOU.
IT WAS FAR HARDER THAN I EXPECTED.
US DOING BATTLE WOULD ONLY BENEFIT CAO CAO.

AND SO?
DID YOU FORGET THE BET HE MADE?

HE SAID HE'D TAKE NANJUN IN LESS THAN A DAY. HE FAILED TO DO SO, SO WE TOOK IT.
MY LORD GOT CARRIED AWAY, THAT'S ALL. HE DIDN'T KNOW HE WAS MAKING A WAGER. YOU CAN'T HOLD THAT AGAINST HIM.

THIS IS SO PETTY OF YOU, BEI LIU! DO YOU REMEMBER THE BATTLE WE JUST WAGED? CAO CAO WAS DOING BATTLE WITH YOU AS MUCH AS QUAN SUN, YET IT WAS OUR SOLDIERS WHO DID THE FIGHTING AND WON THE BATTLE.
AND THEN YOU TURN AROUND AND OCCUPY THESE LANDS?
HOW IS THAT IN ANY WAY FAIR OR JUST?

OOO

HMPH. YOU SPEAK OF THINGS BEING JUST. TELL ME, THESE LANDS BELONGED TO BIAO LIU, YES? WHO LEFT THEM TO BEI LIU, YES?
AND BEI LIU TOOK OVER JINGZHOU AS A FAVOR TO HIS NEPHEW, BIAO LIU'S SON, YES? SO WHAT'S THE PROBLEM?

I WON'T BELIEVE YOU DID IT ONLY TO HELP YOUR NEPHEW UNLESS I HEAR IT FROM HIS MOUTH. WHERE IS QI LIU?

I'M SORRY, I HEARD MY NAME MENTIONED? HELLO, SU LU...

LIANG ZHUGE IS RIGHT. I'VE ASKED MY UNCLE TO TAKE OVER JINGZHOU.

MY LORD QI LIU!

SO YOU SEE, QUAN SUN REALLY HAS NO SAY IN A FAMILY MATTER.

LATER, BACK AT YU ZHOU'S CAMP...
WHAT ARE YOU TALKING ABOUT?
OF COURSE WE HAVE A SAY IN WHO CONTROLS THESE LANDS.
JINGZHOU WAS ALMOST IN OUR HANDS! WE CAN'T LOSE IT LIKE THIS! WE'LL FIGHT FOR IT IF WE HAVE TO.
MY LORD! DON'T GET WORKED UP AGAIN.
THEN WHAT DO WE DO?
YOU SAW BEI LIU'S ARMY. YOU KNOW HOW STRONG HIS FORCES ARE. WITH THAT ARMY AND LIANG ZHUGE BY HIS SIDE, WE CAN'T JUST RUSH INTO A FIGHT.
BY ALL MEANS, OFFER AN ALTERNATIVE TO A FULL-SCALE BATTLE!

I KNEW IT. NO ONE HAS ANY IDEA.
LIANG ZHUGE...
GAH!
UGH...
I WILL KILL THAT--
BE CALM. YOU NEED TO REST.

DON'T WORRY. QI LIU'S DAYS ARE NUMBERED. WHEN HE DIES, BEI LIU WILL LOSE HIS CLAIM TO JINGZHOU. WE CAN FORCE HIM TO HAND IT OVER THEN.
HE'S RIGHT. AND IF THEY EVEN THINK OF TRYING TO TALK THEIR WAY OUT OF IT, I'LL LEAD THE ATTACK MYSELF. THIS WILL BE RESOLVED ONE WAY OR THE OTHER.

SO BE IT.

Chapter 3

Bei Liu Takes Control of JingZhou 209 AD

Summary

Bei Liu, occupying the northern part of JingZhou and acting on advice from Liang Zhuge, orders his men to conquer four southern prefectures of the province. Fei Zhang, Yu Guan, and Yun Zhao are put in command of the armed forces, and during the course of fighting Yu Guan shows respect to an elder soldier, Zhong Huang, that will pay dividends later on. Following the capture of the four prefectures, Bei Liu assumes total control of JingZhou following the death of his nephew, Qi Liu. However, Bei Liu worries about the promise he made to turn over JingZhou to Quan Sun once his nephew died.

Meanwhile, Cao Cao remains in the north, recovering from his defeat at the Red Cliffs. During this time, his second son, Pi Cao, begins acting on his ambition to one day take over for his father. Along with a new advisor, Yi Sima, Pi Cao pays a visit to his brother, Zhi, to get a better sense of whether his brother will one day become his adversary.

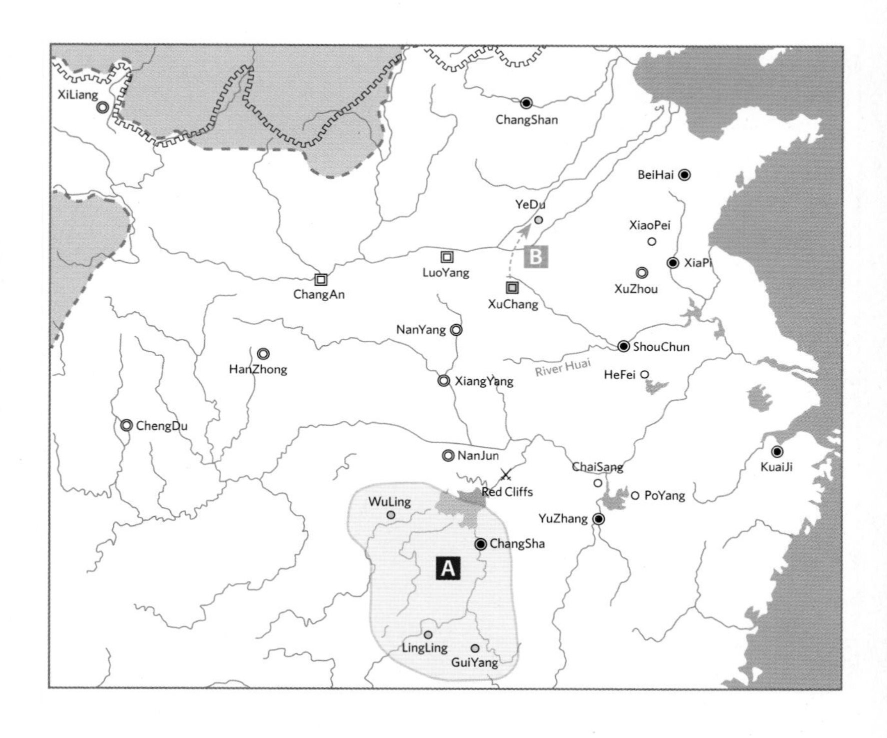

A Bei Liu conquers four southern prefectures of JingZhou and later assumes full control of the province.

B Cao Cao remains in YeDu, where he's still rebuilding after the defeat at the Red Cliffs.

In the spring of 209 AD, Bei Liu made a play for four different southern territories.
Fei Zhang took the lead and conquered LingLing, while Yun Zhao captured GuiYang.
Fei Zhang then went on to claim WuLing, while Yu Guan led an attack against ChangSha.
Yu Guan ended up with the most difficult task, as Commander Zhong Huang was adamant about defending ChangSha.
KLANG

YOU DON'T
HAVE MANY DAYS
LEFT, OLD MAN!
SUBMIT TO THE
INEVITABLE!
ZHONG
HUANG
I MAY BE OLD,
BUT MY EXPERIENCE
IS ENOUGH TO KILL
A CHILD LIKE
YOU!

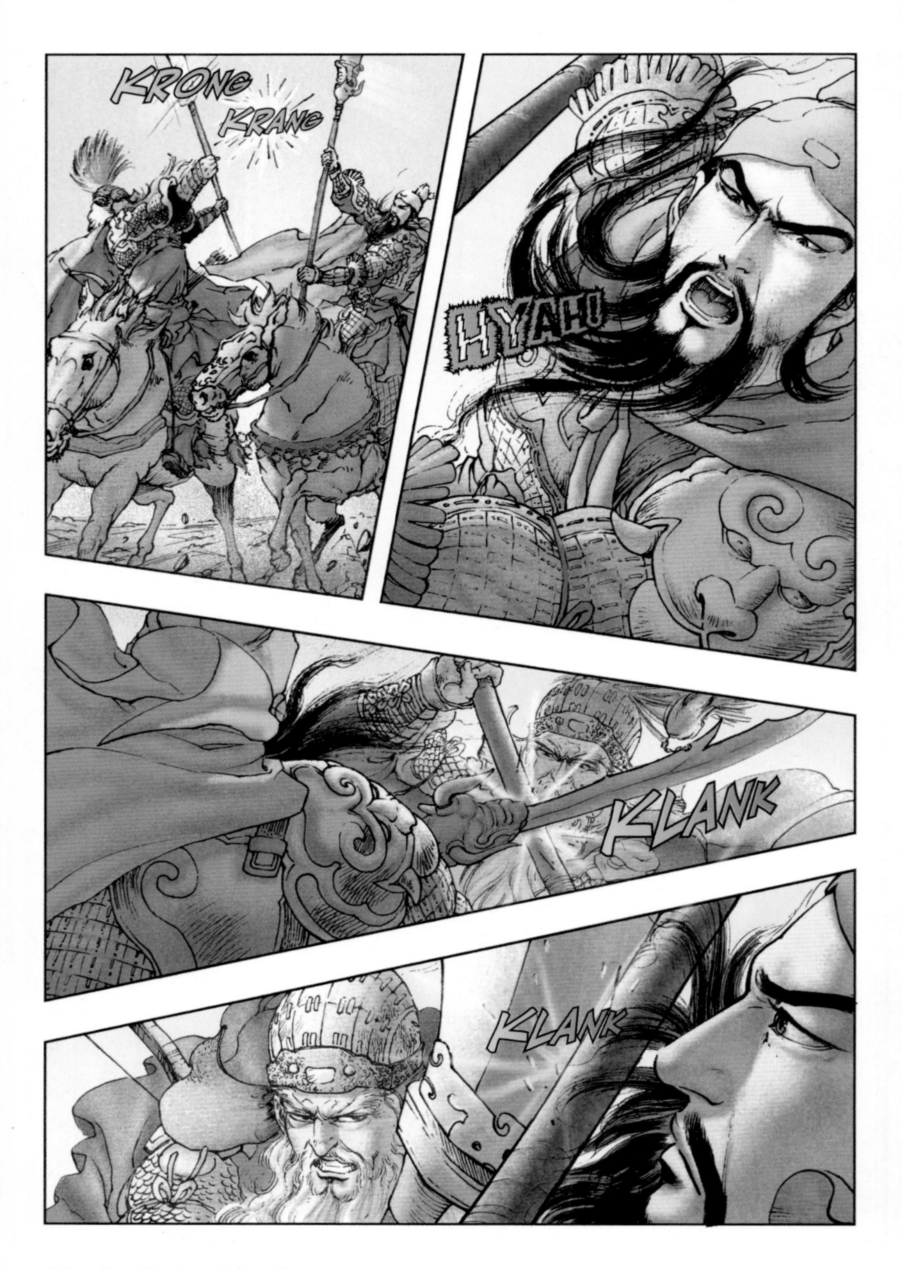
KRONG
KRANG
HYAH!
KLANK
KLANK

WHAM
SHOOM
WHOOSH
KLANG
KRONG
HRAH!

NYEEHH
KLANK
WHOMP

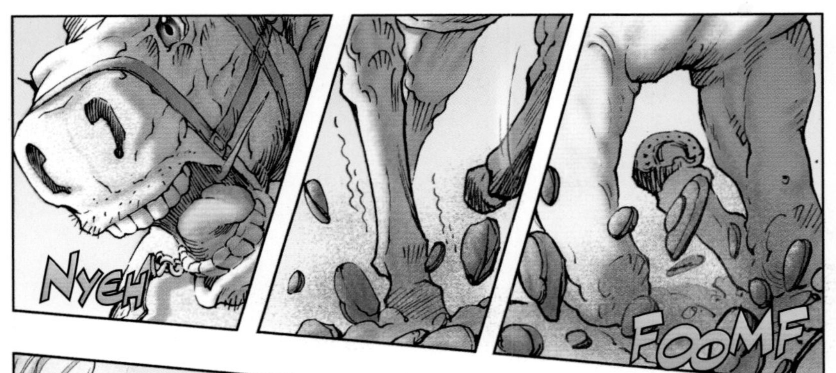
NYEH
FOOMF

THUD
WHOMP

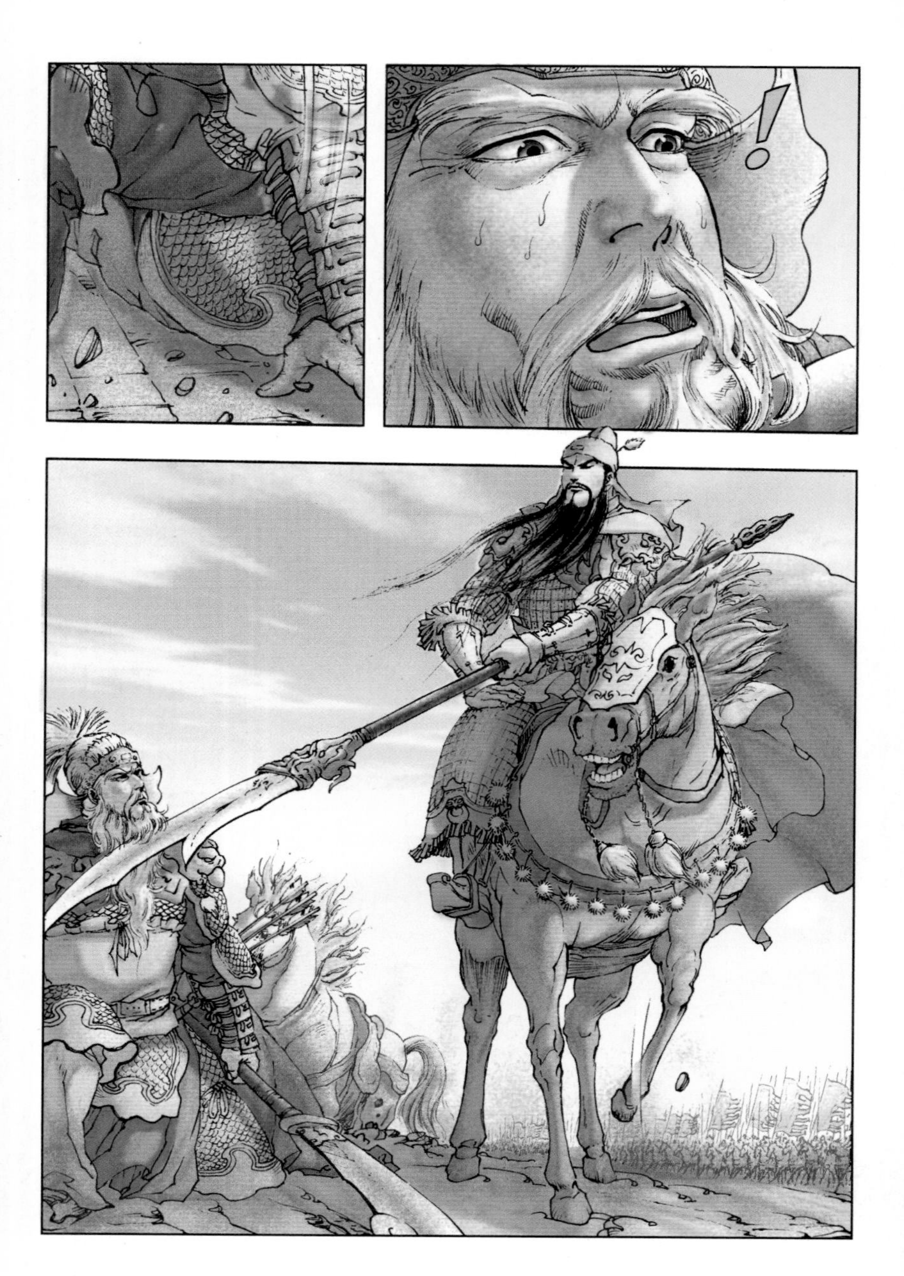

DO IT. I'M READY.

I WON'T KILL A MAN, YOUNG OR OLD, WHO'S BEEN THROWN FROM HIS HORSE.

!

MY LORD!
TAKE THIS HORSE!
CLOP CLOP

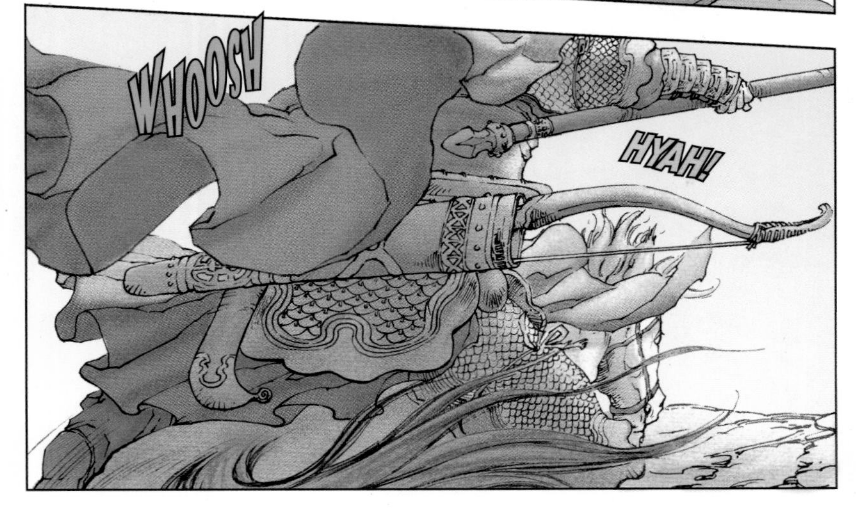
WHOOSH
HYAH!

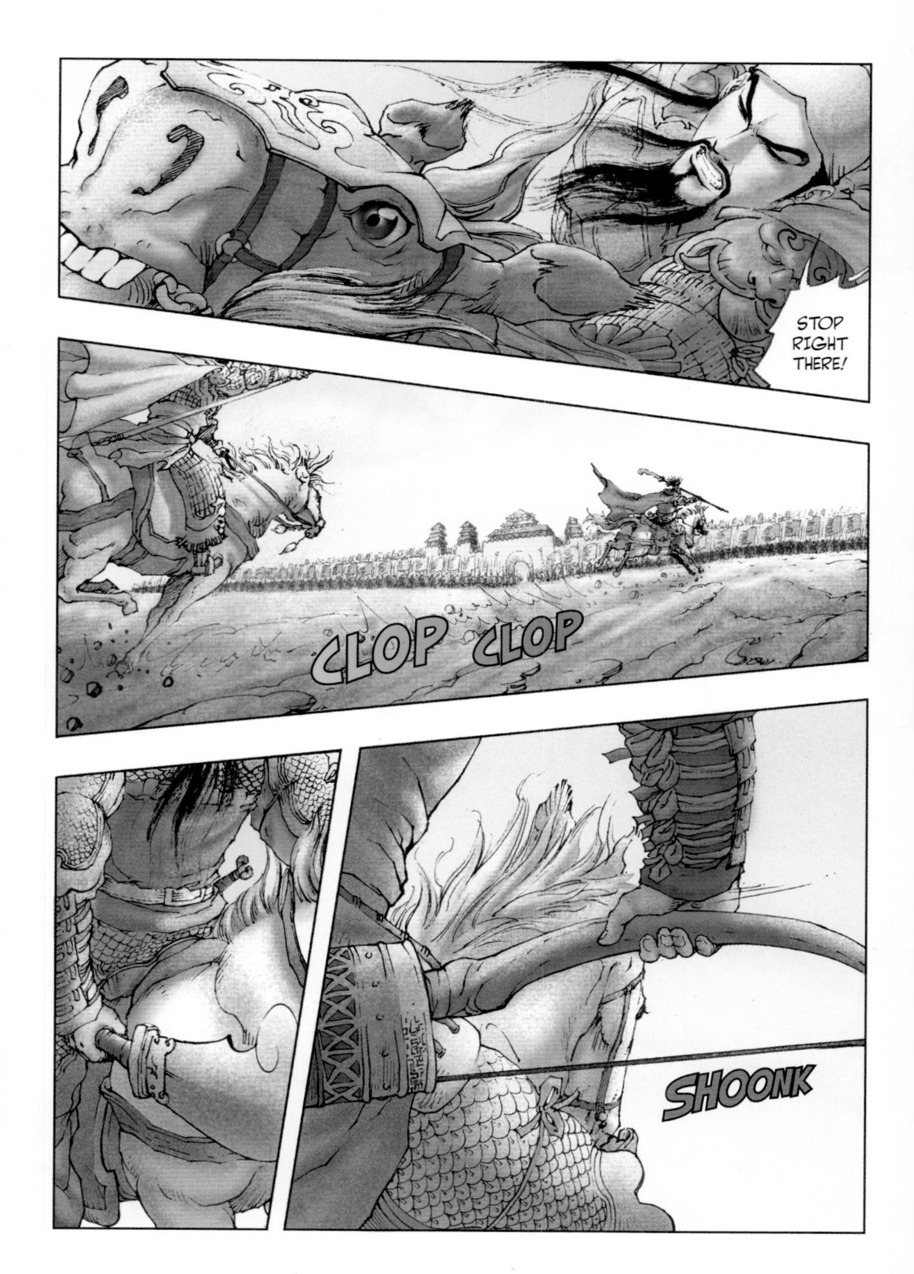
STOP RIGHT THERE!
CLOP CLOP
SHOONK

CLOSER...
CLOP
CLOP

DON'T MAKE ME LAUGH! DO YOU REALLY THINK THAT I, YU GUAN, WILL BE FELLED BY AN OLD MAN'S ARROW?
KREEK
TWANG

ZHING
HOLD UP!
WHOA!

THAT'S ENOUGH FOR ONE DAY, COMMANDER YU GUAN!

I'D SAY THIS MAKES US EVEN FOR NOW.
LET US SEE WHAT HAPPENS TOMORROW, YES?

HE MISSED ON PURPOSE. HE COULD HAVE EASILY SHOT ME IN THE EYE. IF HE WANTED ME DEAD, I WOULD BE BY NOW...

LATER, ZHONG HUANG WAS INTERROGATED BY THE GOVERNOR OF CHANGSHA.
WHY ARE YOU DOING THIS TO ME?
MY LORD, WHAT HAVE I DONE WRONG?
TELL ME, PLEASE!
NO, YOU TELL ME, ZHONG HUANG! TELL ME WHY YU GUAN DIDN'T KILL YOU WHEN YOU WERE THROWN FROM YOUR HORSE. AND TELL ME WHY YOU FAILED TO SHOOT HIM DOWN WHEN YOU HAD THE CHANCE!

XUAN HAN
I THINK YOU ARE COLLUDING WITH YU GUAN! I THINK YOUR FIGHTING AGAINST HIM WAS AN ACT! AM I RIGHT?
NO, MY LORD, OF COURSE NOT! IT'S NOT TRUE!
HMPH.
YOUR BEING ALIVE IS PROOF YOU'RE LYING!
BUT THE LIES END HERE. CUT OFF HIS HEAD AND MOUNT IT ON THE GATE!
NO! YOU CAN'T! THIS ISN'T FAIR!

HRAH!
GRUH!
ENOUGH! THIS MADNESS STOPS RIGHT NOW. GENERAL HUANG IS A NOBLE PROTECTOR OF THESE LANDS.

IT IS YOU, XUAN HAN, WHO IS THE TRAITOR. YOU CANNOT JUST KILL INNOCENT PEOPLE!
YOU HAVE TERRORIZED YOUR PEOPLE LONG ENOUGH! TODAY I WILL MOUNT YOUR HEAD ON THE GATES OF THE CITY!
YAN WEI
YAN WEI, YOU'RE INSANE!
DRAW YOUR SWORDS IF YOU WISH TO FOLLOW YAN WEI!
HE'S RIGHT, THOUGH.
LET'S DO THIS!

TO ARMS!
DRAW!

WELL, XUAN HAN? IT'S YOUR MOVE.

YOU LITTLE WEASEL! HOW DARE YOU BETRAY THE MAN WHO TOOK YOU IN?
DO NOT SPEAK TO ME OF BETRAYAL!
MY LOYALTY IS TO THE PEOPLE, FOR WHOM YOU MUST DIE!

Some time later,
Bei Liu assumed control of JingZhou
when his nephew Qi Liu died.

IT'S SUCH A TERRIBLE SHAME. HE WAS MUCH TOO YOUNG TO DIE. HIS FATHER WILL REFUSE TO LOOK AT ME IN THE AFTERLIFE FOR LETTING THIS HAPPEN.

SIGH
MY LORD, QI LIU'S DEATH WAS NOT SOMETHING WE COULD CONTROL. YOU SHOULDN'T FEEL GUILTY ABOUT SOME-THING THAT WAS DECIDED BY THE HEAVENS.

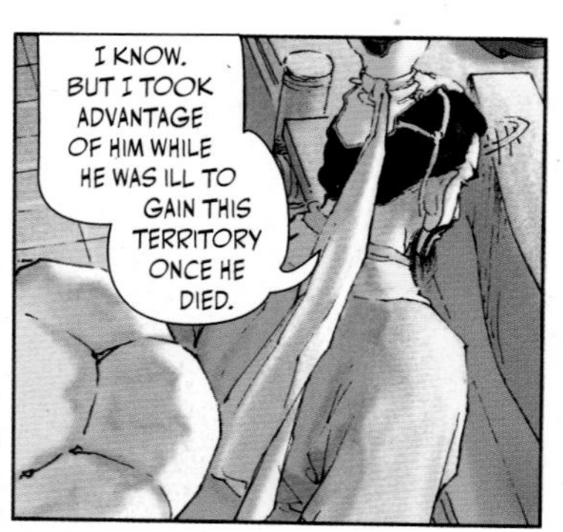

I KNOW. BUT I TOOK ADVANTAGE OF HIM WHILE HE WAS ILL TO GAIN THIS TERRITORY ONCE HE DIED.

ON THE CONTRARY, JINGZHOU BELONGS TO THE HAN DYNASTY, TO YOUR ROYAL FAMILY. IF IT FALLS INTO CAO CAO'S OR QUAN SUN'S HANDS, IT WOULD BE A DEVASTATING BLOW TO YOUR PLANS.
YOU'RE QUITE RIGHT.

BUT THERE WAS THE PROMISE I MADE TO QUAN SUN LONG AGO.
TO RETURN THIS LAND WHEN QI LIU DIED.
YES, I REMEMBER.
LEAVE THAT TO ME.
I'LL MAKE SURE THAT EASTERN WU NEVER SAYS A WORD ABOUT THIS PLACE.

Meanwhile, Cao Cao's son, Zhi, received an unexpected visit from his brother, Pi.

PLEASE, PLEASE!
DON'T STAND UP!

SIT BACK DOWN!
DON'T WANT TO STRAIN YOUR FEET! HA HA!

I JUST DROPPED IN TO SAY HELLO.

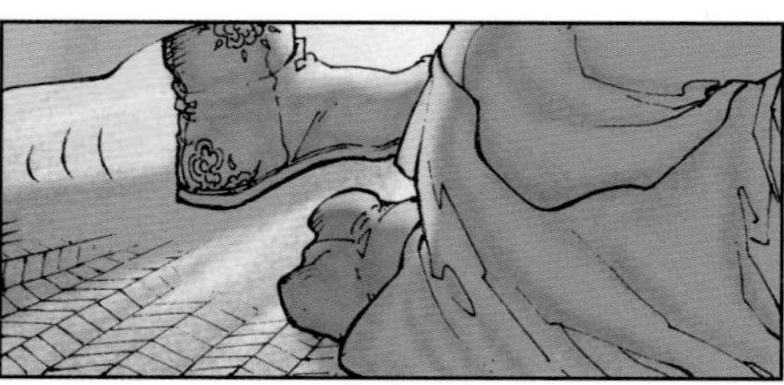

ZHI CAO, I AM MOST IMPRESSED. THIS LOOKS LIKE A GREAT PARTY.

MY LORD, NOW AND THEN WE LIKE TO GATHER THE GREATEST LITERARY MINDS FOR A BANQUET.
LIN CHEN
CAN WANG

AND YOU'VE INVITED THE BEST.
I'M ONLY SORRY THAT RONG KONG DIED BEFORE HE COULD GET THE INVITATION.
PI CAO

PITY. WE'VE LOST SO MANY GREAT MEN.
HMPH.

ZHI CAO!
MANAGE YOUR EMOTIONS, BROTHER. IT IS FAR TOO EASY TO LET GRIEVING CLOUD YOUR JUDGMENT WHEN CONDUCTING STATE AFFAIRS.

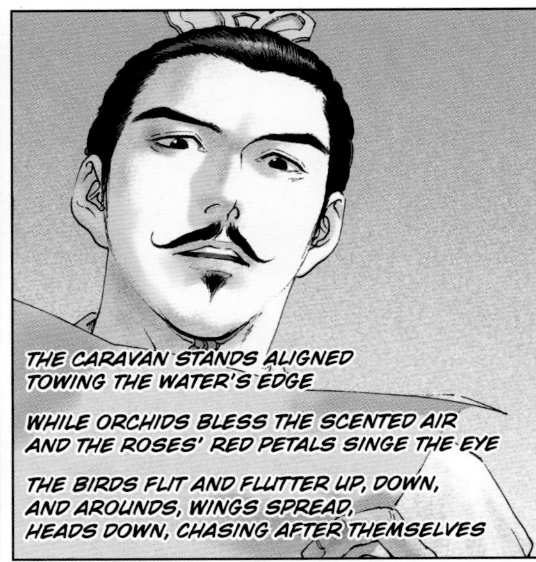
THE CARAVAN STANDS ALIGNED
TOWING THE WATER'S EDGE
WHILE ORCHIDS BLESS THE SCENTED AIR
AND THE ROSES' RED PETALS SINGE THE EYE
THE BIRDS FLIT AND FLUTTER UP, DOWN,
AND AROUNDS, WINGS SPREAD,
HEADS DOWN, CHASING AFTER THEMSELVES

THIS IS AN AMAZING POEM.
NETS CAST FAR AND WIDE
HARPOONS READY FOR THE CARP
AS THE SUN DISAPPEARS INTO THE WEST,
DOES ANYONE CARE IF IT RETURNS?

MASTER CAN WANG, THIS IS YOURS? INCREDIBLE.

YOU ARE KIND TO SAY SUCH THINGS, MY LORD.

MASTER LIN CHEN! IT'S BEEN AGES!

IT'S BEEN, WHAT, YEARS SINCE I LAST SAW YOU IN PERSON? JUST THE SAME, I CAN RECITE YOUR POEMS FROM MEMORY.

WHY, THANK YOU!

MAY I TAKE A LOOK AT THIS?

THE SOUTHERN WIND BLOWS
THE WESTERN SUN GLOWS
MY LOVER HAS OFFERED TO STAY
AND FEAST ON THE REST OF THE DAY
AS I STROLL PAST THE SPRING
MY HEART OFFERS A SIGH
AS THE TREES POINT THE WAY TO MY PLACE IN THE SKY

AMAZING!
THIS POEM TOUCHES MY HEART.
I'M FLATTERED TO HEAR THAT.

MY LORD PI CAO SEEMS TO HAVE A GREAT DEAL OF INTEREST IN POETRY. BUT I WONDER IF HE IS MORE THAN JUST A READER.
XIU YANG

WOULD IT BE TOO MUCH TO ASK MY LORD TO RECITE AN ORIGINAL PIECE?

YOU ARE QUITE EAGER.
MAY I ASK YOUR NAME?
I CAN'T QUITE PLACE YOU...

MY NAME IS XIU YANG. I AM A CLERK FOR YOUR FATHER.

OF COURSE!
YOU ARE DEZU YANG. MY FATHER SPEAKS VERY HIGHLY OF YOU. FORGIVE ME. I DIDN'T RECOG-NIZE YOU.

I HAVE A FEW VERSES COMPOSED IN MY HEAD, BUT I ASK YOU TO NOT EXPECT MUCH.

WOULD YOU MIND JOTTING THIS DOWN?

YI SIMA
NOT AT ALL.

LET'S SEE...

ATOP THE ROCK, AMONG THE STARS,
THERE STANDS A BEACON,
A BLAZING COPPER COMET DECREED BY MAN
IT IS THE ENVY OF ALL
WHO PASS THROUGH THIS REALM,
THEIR COVETOUS NEED GROWING
WITH EACH STEP
BUT SHOULD THEY APPROACH,
THEY WILL BE MET BY THE SPEAR,
FOR HEYANG IS RESERVED FOR
THE FEW

WELL DONE, MY LORD! WELL DONE!
CLAP CLAP
EACH LINE IS EXECUTED WITH TREMENDOUS FEELING AND PRECISION.
CLAP CLAP
THAT IS A MOST DIFFICULT THING TO ACHIEVE.

THAT'S KIND OF YOU TO SAY. BUT I'M NOT THE POET IN THE FAMILY. I THINK ZHI CAO SHOULD OFFER A POEM IN RESPONSE.

THAT'S A GREAT IDEA!
THERE IS NOTHING LIKE A DUEL BETWEEN SIBLINGS.
COME, MY LORD!
A POEM! WE'LL JOT IT DOWN FOR YOU.

VERY WELL...

THE BANQUET IS OVER
AND THE MICE SCRAMBLE
FOR THE CRUMBS FROM THE TABLE
THE MOON BATHES THE ACRES
THAT KNOW NO BOUNDARY OR BORDER
A CHILL RENDS THE AIR
A COLD SHADOW CROSSES THE LAND
GRADUALLY SCATTERED
UNDER THE PALE NIGHT
BENEATH THIS COLD CANOPY OF
AUTUMN FLOAT FLORAL HUES ON
TURQUOISE PONDS
THE FISH PIERCE THE SURFACE
OF THE WATER
AN AUDIENCE RAPT AT THE SOUND
OF BIRDSONG
WHILE A FRIGID WISP OF WINTER
BLOWS FALLEN LEAVES
ALONG THE MENDING GRASS
GONE FROM THE TREES,
GONE FROM THE MEMORY
MAY A THOUSAND AUTUMNS
HAPPEN THUS

WONDERFUL. ABSOLUTELY WONDERFUL.
AN EXTRAORDINARY POEM, MY LORD!

HM...

HM...
YOUR POEM HAS STRUCK US SPEECH-LESS.

WHAT IS THERE TO SAY WHEN HE HAS ALREADY GIVEN VOICE TO THE DIVINE?
CLAP CLAP
INDEED, HIS POEM FELT AS IF IT WAS COMPOSED IN THE LANGUAGE OF THE HEAVENS.

WELL, LET'S NOT GET TOO CARRIED AWAY. IT WAS ONLY A POEM.

REMEMBER THAT OUR FATHER ASKS US TO HELP HIM WITH DEEDS. AND NOT JUST WORDS.

ACTUALLY, YOUR FATHER IS QUITE TAKEN WITH ZHI CAO'S INPUT. HE WAS MOST PLEASED WITH MY LORD'S ANALYSIS OF WHAT WENT WRONG AT THE BATTLE OF THE RED CLIFFS.
THAT IS PART OF THE REASON FOR THE BANQUET TONIGHT.
IS THAT SO?

AND WHAT QUALIFIES A POET TO OFFER SUCH ANALYSIS?
THE ABILITY TO MAKE IT RHYME?

I HAVE A BETTER IDEA. ALLOW ME TO INTRODUCE YI SIMA.

I HAVE BEEN TRAINING UNDER HIM FOR SOME TIME, AND NOW YOU WILL DO THE SAME. I THINK YOU WILL FIND HIM TO BE A SKILLED THINKER.

YI SIMA...
IF I'M NOT MISTAKEN, WASN'T HE ONCE FATHER'S HORSE KEEPER?
HE MUST BE A TRULY SKILLED THINKER. I CAN THINK OF NO OTHER REASON WHY YOU'D LISTEN TO A STABLE-HAND.

YI SIMA WAS WORKING THE STABLES AS PUNISHMENT FOR AVOIDING CIVIL SERVICE. ONCE THERE, THOUGH, HE SAW THE ERROR OF HIS WAYS.
BE MINDFUL OF THAT CON-DESCENDING TONE, BROTHER.

WELL, THEN. IF HE'S AS GIFTED AS YOU SAY, LET HIM ANALYZE THE BATTLE OF THE RED CLIFFS. I'D LOVE TO HEAR WHAT HE HAS TO SAY ABOUT IT.

I...

DON'T BE SHY, YI SIMA. THESE MEN SPEND ALL THEIR DAYS RECITING POETRY. EDUCATE THEM IN MATTERS OF REALITY.

HA HA HA! YES, PLEASE! USELESS MEN SUCH AS WE ARE ALWAYS SITTING AROUND WAITING FOR SOMEONE TO TELL US HOW STUPID WE ARE. PLEASE, TELL US WHAT WE'RE TOO DUMB TO KNOW!

ALL RIGHT, THEN.
THE VICTOR OF THE BATTLE OF THE RED CLIFFS WAS NEVER GOING TO BE EITHER CAO CAO OR QUAN SUN. FROM THE BEGIN-NING, THE ONLY PERSON WHO WOULD EMERGE THE ACTUAL VICTOR WAS BEI LIU.

IS THAT A FACT? THEN EXPLAIN TO ME, HORSEMAN, WHY THE GREATEST SOLDIERS AND STRATEGISTS IN THE LAND ARE FLOCKING TO JOIN THE EASTERN WU--WHO DEFEATED CAO CAO'S MASSIVE ARMY--AND NOT BEI LIU, YOUR SUPPOSED VICTOR.
THE EASTERN WU HAS PROFITED IMMENSELY FROM THE OUTCOME OF THE BATTLE. THIS CANNOT BE DENIED. BUT YOU MEASURE VICTORY IN MORE THAN JUST VISIBLE THINGS; YOU ALSO NEED TO CONSIDER THE VEILED TRUTH.

HAD THE PRIME MINISTER ATTACKED BEI LIU INSTEAD OF FOCUSING HIS ENERGY ON EASTERN WU, HE WOULD NOT HAVE LOST AT THE RED CLIFFS.
BUT HE DIDN'T, GIVING BEI LIU AND LIANG ZHUGE TIME TO TALK QUAN SUN INTO GOING TO WAR WITH US.
SO THE TWO SIDES ENGAGED IN AN ALL-OUT WAR.
WHEN IT WAS OVER, OUR MILITARY STRENGTH WAS GONE.

SO WHAT ARE YOU SAYING?
THAT LIANG ZHUGE PLAYED US FOR FOOLS?

THINK ABOUT IT. WE'VE LOST LITERALLY HUNDREDS OF THOUSANDS OF SOLDIERS, AND QUAN SUN HASN'T GAINED AN INCH OF LAND, EVEN THOUGH HE WON THE BATTLE.

HUH?
UHH...

SIGH
THIS IS POINTLESS. THEY USE THEIR EARS ONLY TO LISTEN TO THEMSELVES.
SO IT WOULD SEEM.

HA HA!
WELL, THAT'S A RELIEF! AND HERE I THOUGHT BATTLES WERE WON AND LOST BY ARMIES! HOW SILLY OF ME.

ENJOY THE REST OF YOUR BANQUET, BUT TRY NOT TO BE UP TOO LATE. WE HAVE ANOTHER BANQUET WITH FATHER TOMORROW.

SURE.

Chapter 4

The Marriage Plot 209 AD

Summary

Following a string of defeats for his army and the untimely death of one of his greatest generals, Ci Taishi, Quan Sun becomes enraged that he has gained almost nothing after the Battle of the Red Cliffs, while Bei Liu has taken over all of JingZhou. Knowing that fighting Bei Liu would require him to ignore the lingering threat of Cao Cao, Quan Sun and Yu Zhou decide to try luring Bei Liu into a deathtrap instead. The bait is a marriage proposal to Quan Sun's younger sister, ShangXiang, an offer that will bring Bei Liu to Eastern Wu, where Yu Zhou can have him killed.

When the proposal arrives, Liang Zhuge sees right through the plot. But rather than fight against Quan Sun, Liang Zhuge advises Bei Liu to accept the marriage proposal. Bei Liu is hesitant, but goes along with the plan. He is escorted to Eastern Wu by Yun Zhao, who has been given a pouch with three sets of special instructions from Liang Zhuge. On the way to meet Quan Sun, Yun Zhao opens the first set of instructions, which tell Bei Liu to announce the impending wedding to anyone he meets. Bei Liu makes a point of meeting, and then inviting to the wedding, every noble and common person he encounters. The result of this is that by the time he meets Quan Sun, Bei Liu is regarded almost as a member of the Sun family by the people of Eastern Wu.

When Quan Sun's mother, Lady Wu, hears of what her son has planned for her daughter, she is enraged. Even if the marriage proposal is a trap, Quan Sun can no longer afford to kill Bei Liu, because to do so would be to make his sister a widow and ruin her life. Lady Wu berates her son and insists on meeting Bei Liu. When she does meet Bei Liu, she is won over by his wisdom and humility, and consents to the marriage. Bei Liu graciously thanks her for her consent, and then asks about the assassins surrounding his cottage...

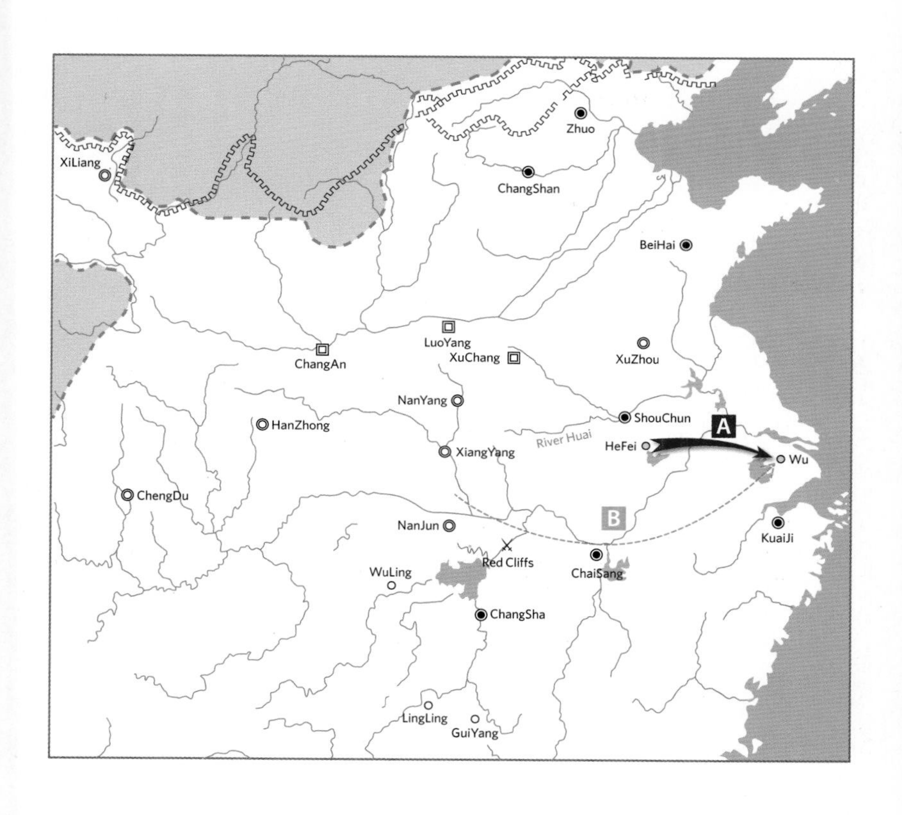

A Quan Sun's army fails to conquer HeFei and returns to Eastern Wu.

B Bei Liu sets out for Eastern Wu to accept the marriage proposal to ShangXiang Sun.

LIAO ZHANG AT THE CITY OF HEFEI
LIAO ZHANG

By the fall of 209 AD, Bei Liu's power had become too great to be neglected. Meanwhile, Quan Sun had launched an attack against HeFei, which was under the protection of Liao Zhang.

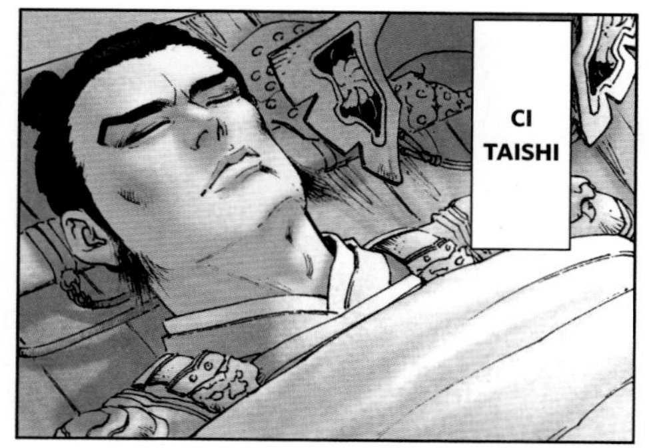
CI
TAISHI

Quan Sun ran into far greater resistance from Liao Zhang than he had expected, and, after an extended battle in which he lost many good men, including Ci Taishi, one of his greatest commanders, Quan Sun was forced to retreat, having gained almost nothing.

QUAN SUN'S CAMP
THESE WERE CI TAISHI'S BLOOD-BOILING LAST WORDS!
"A MAN WHO CHOOSES TO LIVE BY THE SWORD ALSO CHOOSES TO DIE BY THE SWORD. THE ONLY COMFORT LIES IN KNOWING YOU HAVE DIED ACHIEVING SOMETHING GREAT. I FEEL NO SUCH COMFORT, AND DO NOT WISH TO DIE."

SHING

SHAME ON YOU! SHAME ON ALL OF US!
SHONK

HOW MUCH OF OUR PRECIOUS TREASURE HAVE WE SPENT WAGING WAR?
AND I'M NOT JUST TALKING MONEY. I'M TALKING MEN, RESOURCES, AND ENERGY.

WE'VE THROWN EVERYTHING WE HAVE AT THIS.
AND WHERE ARE WE?
WE ARE NOWHERE! WE WON AT THE RED CLIFFS, YET IT IS BEI LIU WHO PROSPERED!

...

WELL?
ANYONE?
HMM...

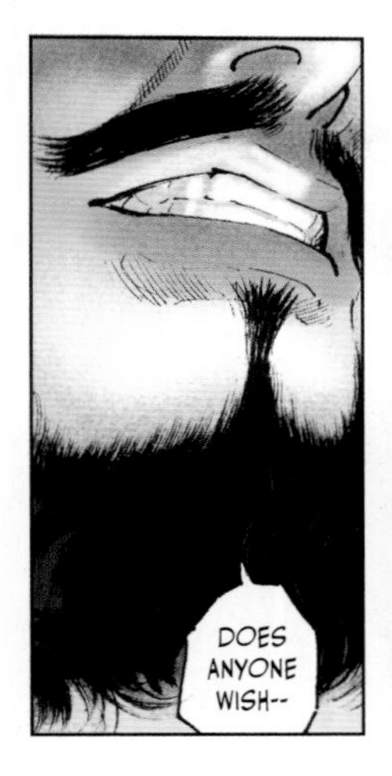
DOES ANYONE WISH--

WE CANNOT DWELL ON THE PAST. WE MUST FOCUS OUR EFFORTS ON THE FUTURE.
NEVER MIND. IT'S NO USE
BEATING A DEAD HORSE.

NOW, THEN...

JINGZHOU IS A STRATEGIC TARGET GOING FORWARD.

WE MUST RECLAIM IT FROM THAT TWO-FACED LIAR, BEI LIU.
FROM THERE, WE CAN BEGIN CLAIMING THE CENTRAL DISTRICTS.
THINK OF THIS AS A FRESH START FOR US.

SO LET US PUT THE PAST BEHIND US.
IT'S A NEW DAY, AND WE HAVE A NEW GOAL.

BUT MARK MY WORDS, I'LL BE KEEPING TRACK OF WHO SCREWS UP.
SO UNLESS YOU WANT TO TASTE MY WRATH, YOU WILL NOT FAIL TO TAKE JINGZHOU. ARE WE CLEAR?

VERY CLEAR, MY LORD. WE'LL ATTACK RIGHT NOW, IF YOU WISH.

WAIT JUST A MINUTE!

MY LORD, LAUNCHING AN OFFENSIVE AGAINST BEI LIU RIGHT NOW WOULD LEAD TO NOTHING BUT ATTRITION FOR BOTH SIDES. THAT WOULD LEAVE US VULNERABLE, EASY FOR CAO CAO TO PREY ON.

HOW ELSE DO YOU EXPECT US TO GET JINGZHOU BACK FROM HIM? BY ASKING POLITELY? WE KNOW HOW EASILY HE GOES BACK ON HIS WORD. WE HAVE NO OTHER OPTION.
MENG LU

WE DON'T HAVE TIME FOR THIS KIND OF DEBATE!
EVERY HOUR WE SPEND NOT FIGHTING TO TAKE BACK JINGZHOU IS AN HOUR LOST!

YU ZHOU?
WHAT DO YOU THINK OF ALL THIS?

FIGHTING WOULD BE A COSTLY DECISION, IT'S TRUE.
NECESSARY, BUT COSTLY. WE SHOULD SEND AN ENVOY FIRST TO SOUND HIM OUT ABOUT THIS.

WHAT GOOD WOULD THAT DO?
BEI LIU KEEPS INVENTING REASONS TO NOT HAND IT OVER. WHY WOULD HE STOP NOW?

SENDING AN ENVOY WOULD BE A FOOL'S ERRAND AT THIS POINT.
NOT EXACTLY, MY LORD.
IF WE SEND AN ENVOY, AND BEI LIU REFUSES TO BUDGE ON JINGZHOU, WE COULD STILL LURE HIM INTO JIANGDONG AND PUNISH HIM ONCE HE'S THERE.

YOU MEAN SET A TRAP FOR HIM HERE?
HM...
BEI LIU IS NOT EASILY LURED. YOU SURE THIS TRAP WILL WORK?

I AM.
WE JUST NEED THE RIGHT BAIT.

OH?

BEI LIU'S CAMP
COMMANDER SU LU, WE'VE BEEN OVER THIS.
WHY DO YOU CONTINUE TO MAKE UNREASONABLE DEMANDS?

WHAT DO YOU MEAN?

SINCE EMPEROR GAOZU WON THE THRONE, THE NATION HAS BELONGED TO THE HAN DYNASTY. A DYNASTY RULED BY BEI LIU'S FAMILY.
I KNOW THAT THINGS HAVE GOTTEN CONFUSED LATELY, WHAT WITH PEOPLE CLAIMING ANYTHING THEY'D LIKE. BUT WE ARE NOT INTERESTED IN TEARING APART THIS NATION ANY MORE.

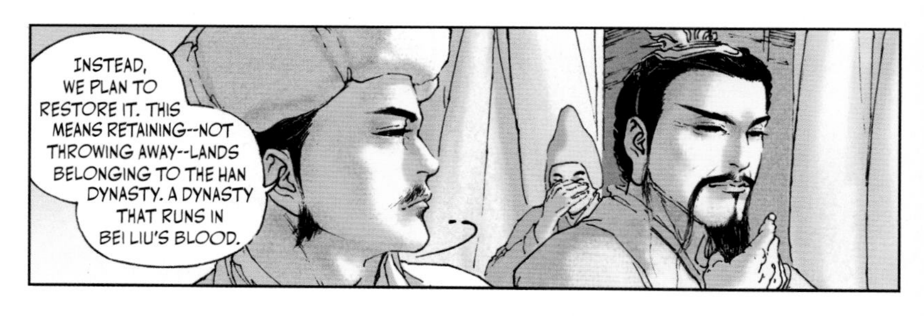
INSTEAD, WE PLAN TO RESTORE IT. THIS MEANS RETAINING--NOT THROWING AWAY--LANDS BELONGING TO THE HAN DYNASTY. A DYNASTY THAT RUNS IN BEI LIU'S BLOOD.

IN OTHER WORDS, JINGZHOU BELONGS TO HIS FAMILY.
SO OF COURSE HE'S GOING TO KEEP CONTROL.
WHY DO YOU KEEP ASKING HIM TO GIVE UP WHAT'S HIS?

I...

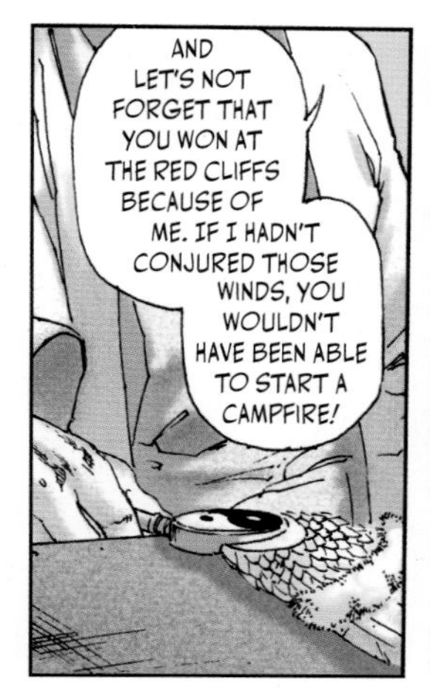
AND LET'S NOT FORGET THAT YOU WON AT THE RED CLIFFS BECAUSE OF ME. IF I HADN'T CONJURED THOSE WINDS, YOU WOULDN'T HAVE BEEN ABLE TO START A CAMPFIRE!

AND IF YOU'D LOST AT THE RED CLIFFS, YOU CAN BET CAO CAO WOULD BE RANSACKING YOUR HOMELAND EVEN AS WE SPEAK. YOUR LANDS AND YOUR FAMILY WOULD NOT ESCAPE HARM!
BY ALL MEANS, STOP ME IF I'M WRONG.

MY LORD, YOUR CLAIM OF OWNERSHIP MAY BE TRUE. BUT TRY TO SEE THINGS FROM MY SIDE. WHEN YOU WERE IN A BIND, IT WAS I WHO ADVISED YU ZHOU NOT TO ALLY WITH CAO CAO.
SIGH THIS SCOLDING IS UNCALLED FOR.

IF YOU REFUSE TO CONSIDER RETURNING IT, WHAT AM I SUPPOSED TO TELL MY MASTER?
IT WAS I WHO CONVINCED YU ZHOU NOT TO ATTACK JINGZHOU. IT WAS I WHO ALSO CONVINCED YU ZHOU YOU WOULD KEEP TO YOUR WORD AND RETURN JINGZHOU.

UNDER-STAND, I'M NOT SAYING I'M AFRAID OF BEING PUNISHED. I DON'T FEAR DEATH.
ALL I'M SAYING IS THAT IF YOU DISMISS ME OUT OF HAND, THEN YOU WILL FIND IT VERY DIFFICULT TO HANG ONTO JINGZHOU. AND I WON'T BE ABLE TO STOP YU ZHOU.

YOU KNOW, WHEN I LOOK AT THE ENORMOUS ARMY THAT WE'VE BUILT UP OVER TIME, I FIND IT DIFFICULT TO FEAR YU ZHOU.
THAT BEING SAID...

I SEE NO REASON WHY WE CAN'T HELP YOUR CAUSE AND KEEP YOU OUT OF TROUBLE. I'LL WRITE A LETTER TO YU ZHOU.
TELL HIM WE'RE ONLY BORROWING JINGZHOU.
BORROWING? WHAT DO YOU MEAN?

WE'LL SAY THAT BEI LIU PLANS TO RETURN JINGZHOU ONCE HE TAKES XITIAN.
WHAT DO YOU THINK?

I... I CANNOT DECIDE ON THIS RIGHT HERE.

THEN I'M AFRAID YOU MUST RETURN EMPTY-HANDED.
BY ALL MEANS, TAKE YOUR TIME TO DECIDE. WE WON'T BE GIVING THIS PLACE UP ANYTIME SOON.
HA HA!

HA HA!
SO THIS IS WHAT LIANG ZHUGE SAYS HE'S GOING TO DO?
THIS SCRAP OF PAPER WOULDN'T FOOL A CHILD!

INDEED, MY LORD. I EXPECTED TO BE DECEIVED. OF COURSE, I HAD TO ENDURE MANY ORNATE WORDS TO BRING THIS BACK.

HA!
YES, I'M AFRAID THAT LIANG ZHUGE'S GREATEST GIFT IS GAB. HE COULD TALK THE GODS TO DEATH.

A LONG-WINDED MAN IS OFTEN SHORT OF PURPOSE.
LET'S SEE IF HE CAN TALK HIS MASTER OUT OF A FOOL-PROOF DEATHTRAP.

COMMANDER YU ZHOU!
REMEMBER, I HAVE ENTRUSTED YOU WITH FIGHTING THIS WAR. SO IT'S ALL ON YOU.
I WANT THIS OVER IN ONE SHOT.
AND I WON'T TOLERATE FAILURE.

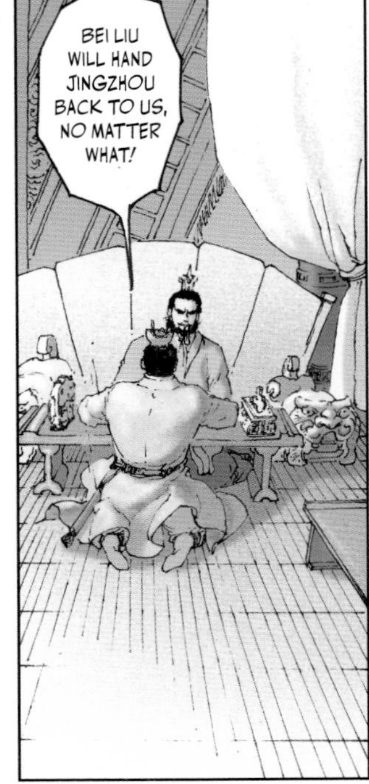
BEI LIU WILL HAND JINGZHOU BACK TO US, NO MATTER WHAT!

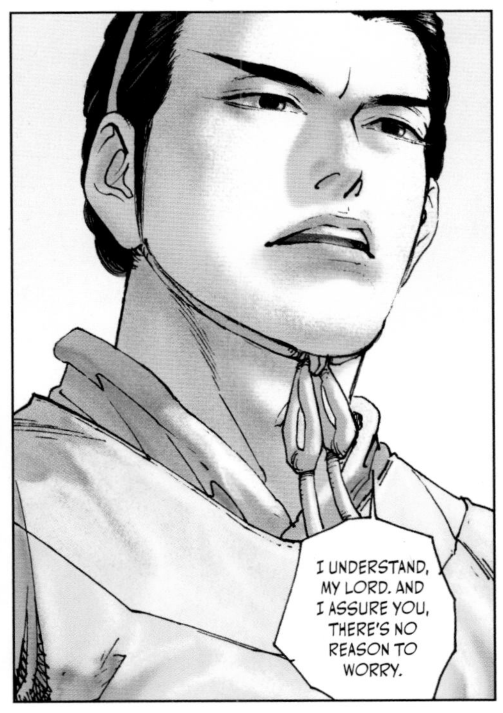
I UNDERSTAND, MY LORD. AND I ASSURE YOU, THERE'S NO REASON TO WORRY.

A short time later, Bei Liu's wife died, and he entered into a period of mourning.

NO DOUBT QUAN SUN HAS READ OUR LETTER BY NOW.
DO YOU THINK THEY'LL BUY OUR STORY?

I GUESS WE'LL HAVE TO ATTACK XITIAN SOON. OTHERWISE, THEY'LL KNOW OUR TRUE INTENTIONS.

THEY ALREADY DO, MY LORD. SU LU CAME HERE ONLY TO SOUND US OUT. HE KNOWS WHAT WE'RE DOING.
WHICH MEANS WE'LL KNOW THEIR TRUE INTENTIONS SOON ENOUGH, AS WELL.

I SUPPOSE THEY COULD RAISE AN EVEN BIGGER ARMY. BUT IF I HAD TO GUESS, I'D SAY THEY'RE GOING TO DEVISE SOME KIND OF SCHEME.

I SEE.

MY LORD!

NEWS FROM QUAN SUN IN EASTERN WU!
SO SOON?

THAT DIDN'T TAKE LONG.

HUH. QUAN SUN OFFERS HIS SYMPATHIES FOR THE LOSS OF MY WIFE... AND HE'S ASKING ME TO TAKE HIS YOUNGER SISTER AS A NEW WIFE!

HA HA HA!

OH, THAT IS PRICELESS! THEY'RE TRYING TO USE A MARRIAGE TRAP TO GAIN BACK JINGZHOU! FUNNIEST THING I'VE HEARD IN AGES.

IT SAYS THEY ARE SENDING AN ENVOY, AND THAT THEY LOOK FORWARD TO STRENGTHENING OUR ALLIANCE.

THIS IS BEYOND UNUSUAL. WHAT ARE WE GOING TO DO?

I JUST LOST MY WIFE. PLUS, I'M MUCH TOO OLD FOR HER. SHE COULD PRACTICALLY BE MY DAUGHTER!

OH, AGE IS SELDOM CONSIDERED IN THESE THINGS. SHE'S OLD ENOUGH TO TAKE YOUR MIND OFF THINGS, IF YOU KNOW WHAT I MEAN.
KNOCK IT OFF. YOU KNOW THIS IS SOME KIND OF MURDER PLOT DEVISED BY YU ZHOU. ARE YOU PLANNING TO FEED ME TO THE WOLVES?

NOT AT ALL. AS USUAL, I'M FIVE STEPS AHEAD OF YU ZHOU.

BELIEVE ME. BY THE TIME I'M DONE DISMANTLING YU ZHOU'S TRAP, YOU'LL HAVE YOUR PICK OF THE SPOILS, BE THEY LAND OR WOMEN!

In the winter of 209 AD,
Quan Sun formally asked Bei Liu to marry his younger sister. Bei Liu accepted the proposal and left JingZhou accompanied by Yun Zhao, who carried three silk pouches given to him by Liang Zhuge.

WELCOME, COMMANDER BEI LIU! YOU HAVE TRAVELED FAR TO HONOR US WITH YOUR PRESENCE.

THE HONOR IS MINE. AND I THANK YOU FOR COMING OUT TO MEET ME IN PERSON.

ALL RIGHT YUN ZHAO, OPEN THE FIRST SILK POUCH THAT LIANG ZHUGE GAVE YOU.

YES, MY LORD.

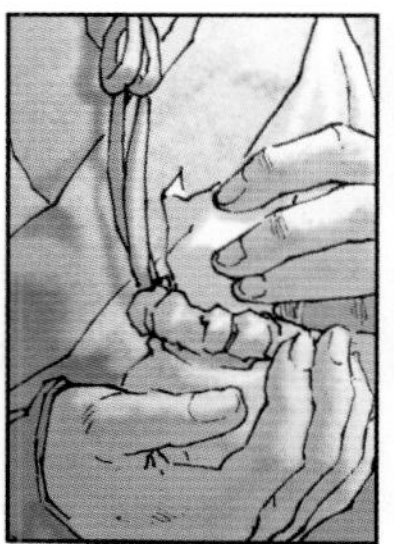

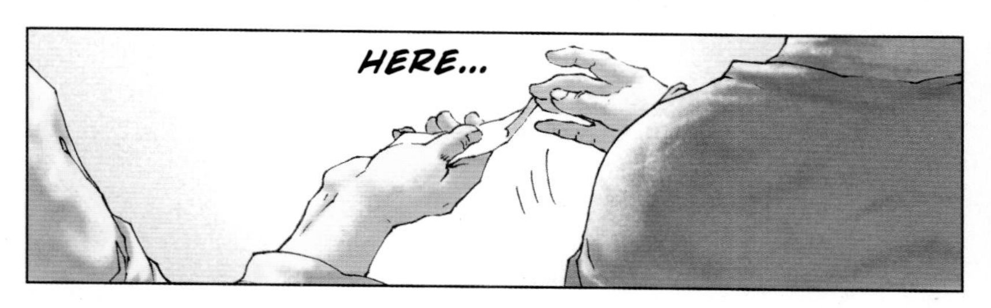
HERE...

HM... I SEE...

ALL RIGHT.
DO AS IT SAYS.

Bei Liu then proceeded to invite every notable person in Eastern Wu to his impending wedding.

TELL ME... IS THERE ANYONE ALONG THE WAY TO THE NEXT NOBLEMAN'S HOUSE WHO MIGHT LIKE TO COME?
OF COURSE THERE ARE!

I'LL BE HAPPY TO INTRODUCE YOU TO THEM, TOO.
I TAKE GREAT PRIDE IN ASSISTING THE DYNASTY.
THIS WAY, MY LORD.

I CAN'T THANK YOU ENOUGH FOR ALL YOUR WORK. I WANT TO MEET AS MANY PEOPLE HERE AS I POSSIBLY CAN! HA HA HA!

THIS IS THE DESIGN PLAN FOR THE COTTAGE WHERE BEI LIU IS STAYING.
Yun Zhao
Bei Liu

WE'VE DESIGNED AN AMBUSH THAT CAN BE LAUNCHED FROM ANY DIRECTION. ONCE IT'S DARK, IT WILL BE POSSIBLE TO TAKE BEI LIU BY COMPLETE SURPRISE.
THE ONLY PART I DON'T LIKE IS THAT YUN ZHAO IS WITH BEI LIU. WE'LL NEED TO COORDINATE OUR MOVEMENTS SO AS TO CAPTURE BOTH MEN WITHOUT A FUSS.

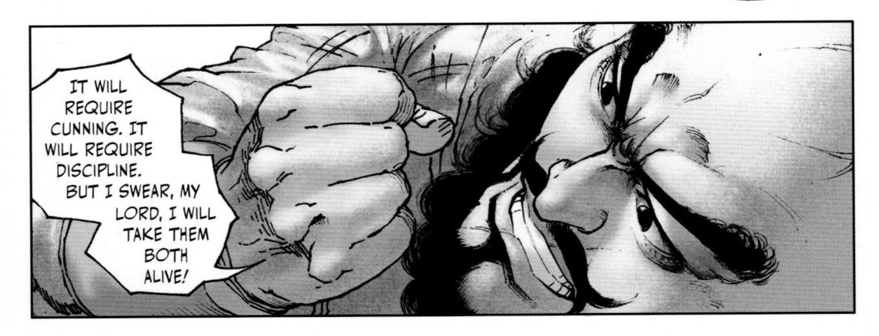
IT WILL REQUIRE CUNNING. IT WILL REQUIRE DISCIPLINE. BUT I SWEAR, MY LORD, I WILL TAKE THEM BOTH ALIVE!

OR YOU COULD KILL THEM. THAT WORKS TOO.
OH. I SEE.
THAT MAKES LIFE EASIER. YES, MY LORD!

THIS IS A GOOD AMBUSH PLAN. UNLESS BEI LIU MANAGES TO...
GROW WINGS, THERE IS NO ESCAPE FOR HIM.

YAWN GOOD WORK.
I THINK I CAN SLEEP PEACEFULLY NOW.
INDEED YOU MAY, MY LORD. WE'VE GOT HIM NOW.
HA HA!

OOF!
THUD
MY LADY, PLEASE!
YOU'RE NOT SUPPOSED TO BE IN HERE!

UNLESS YOU WANT BROKEN FINGERS TO GO WITH THAT BROKEN NOSE, THEN GET THE HELL OUT OF MY WAY AND LET ME SEE MY SON!
LADY WU

MOTH-ER! WHAT BRINGS YOU HERE?

A DISGRACE-FUL SON AND HIS PATHETIC LAP DOG!

SLAP
SLAP

OW! WHAT DO YOU MEAN, MOTHER?

HOW DARE YOU!
I...
AND DON'T CALL ME MOTHER!

STATE ELDER QIAO, YU ZHOU'S FATHER-IN-LAW

WHAT THE HELL IS GOING ON HERE?

WILL SOMEONE TALK TO ME? WHAT ARE YOU SO MAD ABOUT?

WHAT AM I--DON'T PLAY GAMES WITH ME, SON.
YOU SOLD YOUR YOUNGER SISTER IN MARRIAGE, FOOL!
AND YOU DIDN'T EVEN HAVE THE GUTS TO CONSULT ME!

OH.

IT'S NOT WHAT YOU THINK. IT'S JUST A TRAP WE LAID.
WE'RE LURING BEI LIU INTO RETURNING JINGZHOU TO US.

OH, I GET IT...
YOU'RE SAYING THE MAN YOU PUT IN CHARGE OF YOUR MILITARY IS SO USELESS THAT HE HAS TO RESORT TO WHORING OUT YOUR YOUNGER SISTER? BECAUSE HE CAN'T GET THE JOB DONE?

BUT THE MARRIAGE ISN'T GOING TO HAPPEN. ONCE WE'VE CAUGHT BEI LIU, WE'LL CALL OFF THE WEDDING.

HOW, YOU FOOL?
WORD OF THE WEDDING HAS ALREADY SPREAD ACROSS THE LAND.
HOW CAN YOU CALL IT OFF?

WAIT. HOW COULD WORD HAVE SPREAD? WE DIDN'T TELL ANYONE.

NO, YOU DIDN'T. BUT BEI LIU HAS BEEN TRAVELING HIGH AND LOW AND TELLING ANYONE WHO WILL LISTEN ABOUT HIS IMPENDING MARRIAGE. EVEN SMALL CHILDREN ARE EXCITED ABOUT THIS.
THIS IS CRAZY. HOW DO YOU KNOW THIS?

BECAUSE BEI LIU PERSONALLY INVITED ME TO THE WEDDING.
HE'S VISITED ALMOST ALL THE NOBLEMEN AND INVITED THEM TOO.

THIS IS A FANTASTIC MESS YOU'VE CREATED FOR US, DON'T YOU REALIZE THAT? WHAT IS YOUR LITTLE SISTER SUPPOSED TO DO NOW?

IF YOU KILL BEI LIU NOW, YOU'LL MAKE HER A WIDOW, AND SHE'LL HAVE TO SPEND THE REST OF HER LIFE IN MOURNING. HER LIFE WILL BE OVER BEFORE IT'S EVEN HAD A CHANCE TO START!
WHO DOES THIS TO FAMILY? WHAT KIND OF BROTHER OR SON ARE YOU?

SO YOU'LL RECLAIM JINGZHOU BY WAY OF THIS LUDICROUS PLAN. WELL DONE.
TOO BAD THE WORLD WILL LAUGH AT YOU FOR BEING A GUTLESS COWARD!

GAH!

MOTHER!
MY CHEST ACHES!
UGH!

DON'T TOUCH ME!
BUT I...

MY LADY, THE PLAN HAS GONE TOO FAR. AT THIS POINT, YOUR ONLY CHOICE IS TO ACCEPT BEI LIU AS YOUR SON-IN-LAW.

ABSOLUTELY NOT! I WILL NOT ALLOW IT!
OH, SHUT UP!

YOU SAID YOU MET BEI LIU IN PERSON?

I DID. HE'S AN OLDER MAN, THERE IS NO DOUBT. BUT HE IS ALSO A MAN OF WISDOM AND DIGNITY. HE WOULD BE A GOOD MATCH FOR YOUR DAUGHTER.
HMPH.

VERY WELL. I WILL MEET WITH HIM IN PERSON. AND MAKE UP MY OWN MIND.

I'LL BE THE ONE WHO DECIDES IF THIS MARRIAGE PROPOSAL GOES THROUGH OR NOT. UNDER-STOOD?

IF I'M NOT SATISFIED WITH BEI LIU, YOU'RE WELCOME TO DO WHATEVER YOU WANT WITH HIM. BUT IF I DO LIKE HIM...
THEN YOU'RE GOING TO HAVE A NEW BROTHER-IN-LAW!

HRR...

DAMN IT! HOW DID THIS GET SO OUT OF HAND?!
WHOMP

Yu Zhou

IS THERE SOMETHING BOTHERING YOU, COMMANDER YU GUAN?

YOUR HAND IS HERE, PLAYING OUR GAME.

BUT YOUR MIND IS CLEARLY SOMEWHERE ELSE.

BEI LIU IS IN THE ENEMY'S CAMP. YOU DON'T EXPECT ME TO BE ABLE TO SIT HERE AND IDLY PLAY A BOARD GAME, DO YOU?
BUT THAT'S PRECISELY WHY THIS GAME IS IMPORTANT. IT'S LIKE LIFE.
A STONE PLACED ON THE BOARD WITH A CLEAR MIND BECOMES A WEAPON AGAINST YOUR ENEMY.

BUT IF YOUR MIND IS BUSY, IT'LL SHOW WHEN YOU PLACE YOUR ROCK, AND I'LL KNOW YOUR NEXT MOVE.

I KNOW YOU ARE A VERY CLEVER MAN, BUT THERE ARE PITFALLS IN EVERY ASPECT OF LIFE.

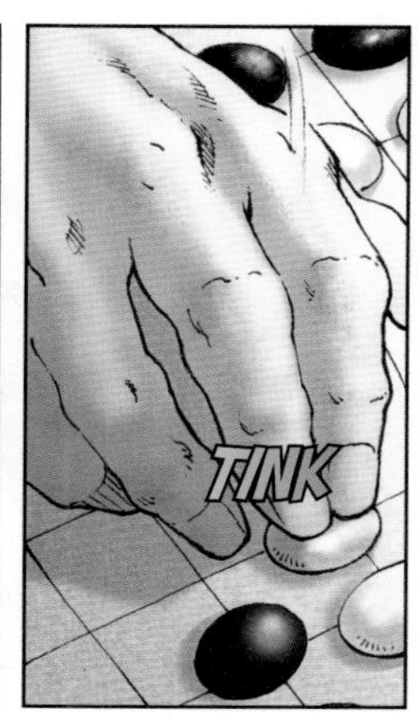
TINK

WHICH IS WHY I ALWAYS TAKE THOSE PITFALLS INTO ACCOUNT.

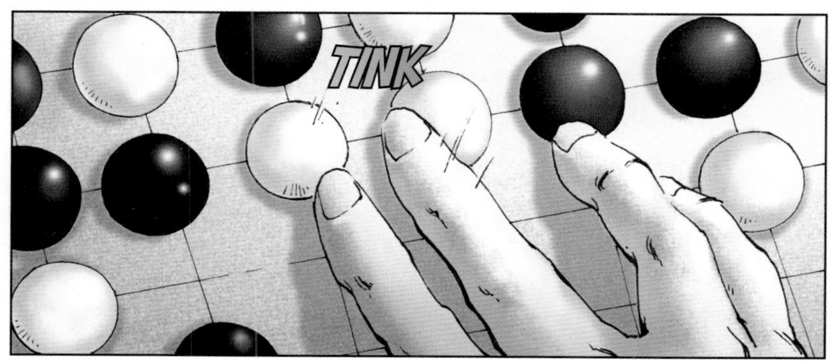
TINK

HUH.
THAT'S A CLEVER MOVE.

I'D SAY THE MATCH IS OVER.

MY LORD!
I HAVE A MESSAGE FROM COMMANDER BEI LIU.

HA HA!

REST EASY, YU GUAN. BEI LIU IS SAFE. HE AND QUAN SUN ARE ALMOST FAMILY NOW!
HA HA HA!
THE NEWS OF BEI LIU'S MARRIAGE IS SPREADING LIKE WILDFIRE.

The rumor of Bei Liu's wedding spread so far and so fast that by the time he climbed the steps to meet Lady Wu, half the province thought he was already family. The scheme Liang Zhuge had devised and placed instructions for in the silk pouches had made the marriage almost an irreversible fact. At this point, Lady Wu could only give her final blessing.

FINALLY...

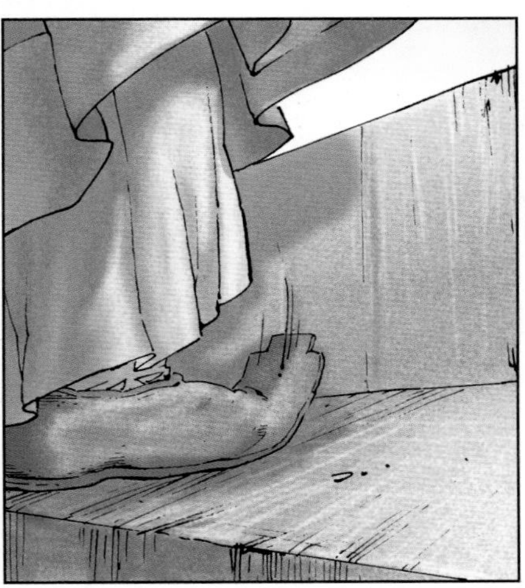

SWEET DEW TEMPLE

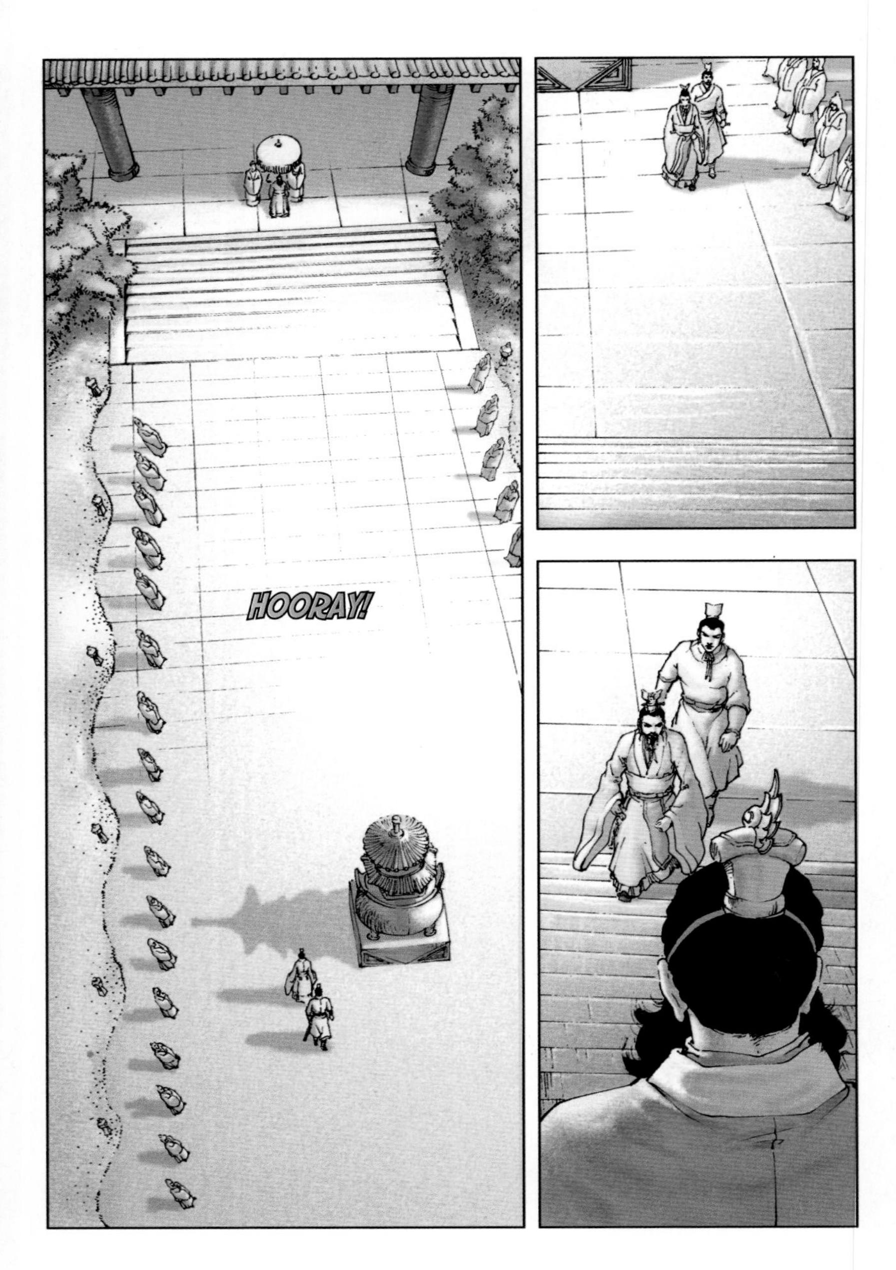
HOORAY!

THIS IS THE GREAT BEI LIU? IMPOSSIBLE! HE LOOKS TOO ORDINARY.

SO THIS IS QUAN SUN... QUITE AN IMPRESSIVE FIGURE.

COMMANDER BEI LIU! IT IS MY GREAT HONOR TO WELCOME YOU TO EASTERN WU.
WE SHOULD HAVE MET UP AFTER THE RED CLIFFS, BUT IT WAS NOT TO BE.
MY LORD QUAN SUN, THE HONOR IS MINE.
TRULY YOU ARE YOUR FATHER'S SON. WHAT DO THEY CALL YOU, THE DRAGON OF THE EAST?

HA HA! I'VE ACHIEVED A FEW THINGS, IT'S TRUE. BUT I DON'T KNOW THAT I'VE EARNED THAT NAME.

AND THIS MUST BE YUN ZHAO. WORD HAS IT YOU FOUGHT YOUR WAY THROUGH CAO CAO'S ARMY WITH NOTHING BUT A SWORD AND A BABY.

YES, MY LORD. IT'S AN HONOR TO MEET YOU.

HA! A MAN OF UNIQUE COURAGE. I CAN SEE IT IN YOUR EYES.

THIS WAY, PLEASE. MY MOTHER IS WAITING FOR YOU.
OH.
OF COURSE.

HUH. HM...

MY LADY WU, I AM HUMBLED TO BE IN YOUR PRESENCE.
MAY YOU ALWAYS KNOW HEALTH AND WISDOM.

PLEASE SIT DOWN.

SO... BEI LIU... YOU CERTAINLY LIVE UP TO YOUR REPUTATION.

YES.
I CAN SEE THE DIVINE IN YOUR EYES.
I GLADLY GIVE MY DAUGHTER TO A MAN AS GREAT AS YOU.

HMPH. ALL I SEE IS A FORMER PEASANT WITH A RUN OF GOOD LUCK.

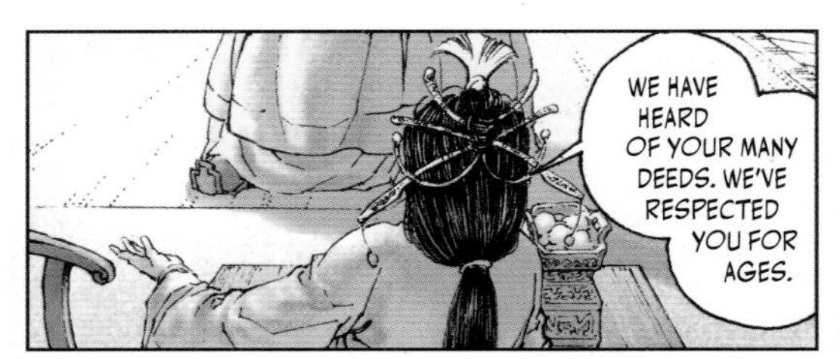
WE HAVE HEARD OF YOUR MANY DEEDS. WE'VE RESPECTED YOU FOR AGES.

MY LADY, I'M JUST A MAN WITH A REPUTATION. YOU, HOWEVER, ARE HEAD OF A FAMILY WHOSE GREATNESS SPANS GENERATIONS.

HA! SO YOU ARE MODEST AND GOOD AT FLATTERY! TWO MORE VIRTUES.

I'VE PREPARED A BANQUET IN YOUR HONOR. PLEASE JOIN ME. I'D LIKE TO KNOW MORE ABOUT MY NEW SON-IN-LAW.

IT WOULD BE MY PLEASURE, MY LADY.

ALL HANDS!
BRING THE DINNER TABLE INTO THE ROOM!

COMMANDER BEI LIU!
I'D LIKE TO MAKE A TOAST.
TO THE NEWEST MEMBER OF OUR GREAT FAMILY. MAY WE DO GREAT THINGS TO-GETHER.

I CANNOT TELL YOU HOW MOVED I AM TO BE WELCOMED INTO YOUR HOME WITH SUCH WARMTH AND CHARITY.
I NEVER EXPECTED SUCH KINDNESS.
TO THE FAMILY OF WU!

IN THE END, IT IS ONLY FITTING FOR US TO HAVE A BLOOD RELATION WITH THE EMPEROR.
DON'T MAKE EXCUSES, AND DON'T BOAST, YOU TWERP. LEARN A THING OR TWO ABOUT MODESTY FROM BEI LIU.

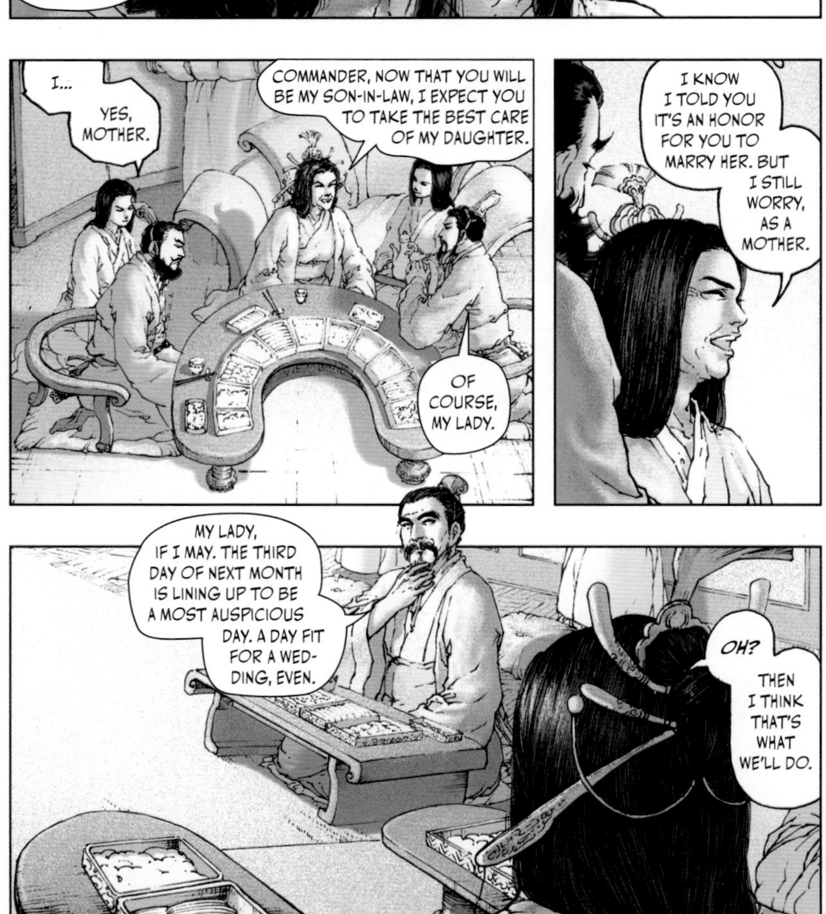
I...
YES, MOTHER.
COMMANDER, NOW THAT YOU WILL BE MY SON-IN-LAW, I EXPECT YOU TO TAKE THE BEST CARE OF MY DAUGHTER.
OF COURSE, MY LADY.
I KNOW I TOLD YOU IT'S AN HONOR FOR YOU TO MARRY HER. BUT I STILL WORRY, AS A MOTHER.
MY LADY, IF I MAY. THE THIRD DAY OF NEXT MONTH IS LINING UP TO BE A MOST AUSPICIOUS DAY. A DAY FIT FOR A WED-DING, EVEN.
OH?
THEN I THINK THAT'S WHAT WE'LL DO.

WHY DID HE? YOU'RE NOT HELPING, YOU MORON.
I LIKE IT.

WHAT DO YOU THINK, SON?

I THINK IT'S PERFECT, MOTHER.
AND *YOU*, BEI LIU?

I HAVE NO OBJECTION TO THE WEDDING DATE. MY ONLY WORRY IS ABOUT THE NEXT DAY.
I FEAR SOMETHING AWFUL MIGHT HAPPEN.

WHAT?

I DON'T UNDERSTAND. WHAT DO YOU MEAN?
WHY SHOULD SOMETHING AWFUL HAPPEN?

MY LADY, I'VE TREATED THIS MARRIAGE PROPOSAL WITH SINCERITY.
BUT I'M NOT THE ONLY ONE INVOLVED.

SIGH
IF YOU WANT TO GET RID OF ME, DO IT. KILL ME, BEFORE WE WASTE OUR TIME WITH THIS.

WHAT ARE YOU TALKING ABOUT?
NOBODY HERE IS GOING TO KILL YOU.
I WANT TO BELIEVE YOU, MY LADY. BUT IF THAT'S TRUE, WHY ARE MY SLEEPING QUARTERS SUR-ROUNDED BY ASSASSINS?

ASSASSINS?

HUH?
WHAP

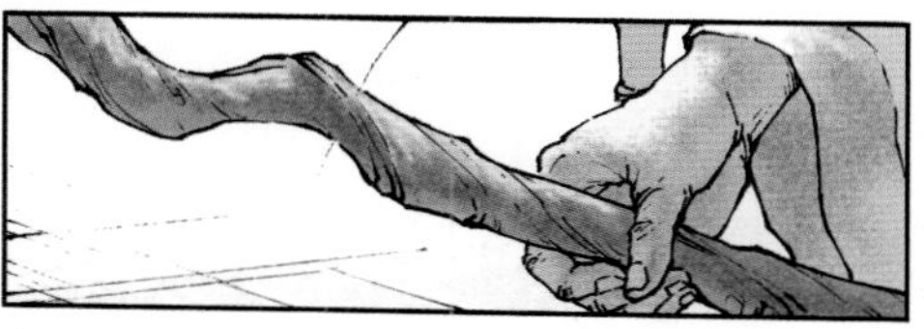

I HAVE NO IDEA! PROMISE!

WHAT IS HE TALKING ABOUT? SPEAK!

FAN LU!
WHERE ARE YOU?
GET IN HERE! RIGHT NOW!

YES, MY LORD!
YOU ARE SPEAKING TO ME, FAN LU. AND YOU WILL ANSWER TRUTHFULLY.

HAVE YOU HIRED ASSASSINS TO KILL BEI LIU?

I...UM...

UN-UH...
WELL... UM...

YOU SEE...

I WAS JUST--

SPEAK UP, YOU IDIOT!

MY MOTHER IS ASKING YOU A QUESTION!
NOW ANSWER HER!
WHO BROUGHT IN THE ASSASSINS TO KILL BEI LIU?!
UM...
WELL...

TRUST BUT VERIFY

Three Kingdoms is a story about the bonds of fidelity, the cost of hubris, and the question of whether war can actually accomplish peace. Furthermore, it is a study of what happens when good people are confronted with stark choices that challenge their honor. But while the story places a great deal of merit in the idea that people are capable of doing the right thing in the end, it is very much preoccupied with depicting the various ways in which people fail – as rulers, as family members, or as those entrusted to help someone win the throne.

While hubris is the greatest factor in the downfall of several characters in Three Kingdoms, trust is the second greatest factor. From the earliest parts of the story, such as when Zhuo Dong put his faith in Bu Lu and Bu Lu put his faith is Diao Chan, various characters have been undone because they placed blind faith in those who were not worthy of their trust. Because, while trust may be an admirable human trait, in Three Kingdoms trust is sometimes just another form of hubris. When you look at it objectively, there is

very little reason for Cao Cao to put so much faith in Tong Pang's plan to chain all of his ships together. But Cao Cao believes that he's had ill fortune since losing his best counselor, and that his failure to trust the advice of his remaining counselors is the reason for the bad luck. So he foolishly accepts the strategy of a complete stranger, because he feels doing so will change his fortunes. In other words, Cao Cao needs to believe he has the power to change his fortune, so he is completely blind to the reality that anyone who approaches him with an offer of help is likely trying to deceive him.

In contrast to Cao Cao, Liang Zhuge has managed to change the course of events on several occasions precisely because he does not trust anyone. This does not make Liang Zhuge a cruel or cynical person. Rather, it means that he trusts his own counsel enough to know that he cannot predict when someone will betray his trust. He just knows when the odds are likely that it will happen, and he plans accordingly. When Liang Zhuge reluctantly dispatches Yu Guan to kill Cao Cao, he knows the mission will fail. Despite Yu

Guan's assurances, Liang Zhuge knows his debt to Cao Cao was not repaid in full, and he knows this will prevent Yu Guan from carrying out his task. But rather than place all his trust in Yu Guan, Liang Zhuge trusts himself and has a plan ready in the event that Yu Guan fails. Unlike Cao Cao, Liang Zhuge is not desperate to assert his dominance over events. As a result, he is better able to predict, and then control, outcomes.

While it is not the nicest of sentiments, being careful when trusting others is a necessary lesson in the story of Three Kingdoms. While the story is not suggesting that people can't be trusted, it does suggest that trust should be coupled with caution, because caution can temper the impulsive nature of trusting someone without hesitation. Those who neglect such caution often find themselves wondering what went wrong.

ZHONG HUANG

CI TAISHI